A LACK OF MOTIVE

David Brunelle Legal Thriller #8

STEPHEN PENNER

ISBN-13: 9780692897706

ISBN-10: 0692897704

A Lack of Motive

Joy A. Lorton, Editor.

Cover by Nathan Wampler Book Covers.

THE DAVID BRUNELLE LEGAL THRILLERS

A LACK
OF MOTIVE

Motive is not an element of murder. Therefore, the State is not required to prove a motive for the commission of the crime charged.

However, if the proof establishes that the defendant had no motive to commit the crime charged, that is a circumstance you may consider as tending to establish that the defendant is not guilty.

People v. Seppi, 221 N.Y. 62 (1917)

CHAPTER 1

Every garden has its serpents.

Homicide D.A. David Brunelle frowned as he took Exit 9 from eastbound I-90 and turned north onto Bellevue Way.

Bellevue.

Brunelle remembered old T.V. shows set in New York where the cops would take the crazy people to 'Bellevue'—the mental hospital in that great metropolis. But on the other side of the continent, in the lesser metropolis of Seattle, Bellevue was an asylum of a different sort. It was the crown jewel of 'The Eastside,' the string of suburbs on the east shore of Lake Washington, separated by that body of water from Seattle proper, connected only by two floating bridges, one of which Brunelle had just finished crossing. Once a sleepy vacation village, Bellevue had grown into a city in its own right, with a skyline of a half dozen 40-story office towers, a nationally ranked school system, and the highest average home price in the state. If you could make it there—well, you'd made it. It was known for money and mansions, not murder.

But, Brunelle considered again as he approached the glass and steel downtown, *gardens and serpents*.

He crossed under the streetlights at Main Street, his tires splashing through the black puddles left over from the day's rain, and looked for the entrance to the parking garage under the latest mixed-use, retail-and-condominium high-rise. It wasn't hard to spot. At one in the morning the streets were deserted, but the patrol car parked at the entrance of the subterranean garage, its emergency lights flashing blue and red, made sure Brunelle didn't miss his turn. He waved to the uniformed officer standing guard next to his vehicle and descended into the cement labyrinth beneath the city.

Brunelle vaguely remembered reading a Greek myth in high school about a Minotaur at the center of a labyrinth, but he couldn't recall if the maze had been empty prior to the hero's arrival at his destination. Still, he was pretty sure the hero hadn't been waved down four levels of parking by uniformed police officers with flashlights. Brunelle repeated his 'thank you' wave to each officer as he passed, circling the garage in silence, as if the weight of the earth above prevented any sound from disturbing the dignity of the tomb the garage had, at least temporarily, become.

The center of the maze finally came into view when he reached level P4. But there was no Minotaur. Unless the Minotaur had been shot in the head while sitting in the driver's seat of a black Audi A4.

Brunelle parked his own, far more modest domestic sedan a few parking spots away from the yellow crime scene tape cordoning off the Audi from the rest of the garage. Then he stepped out and looked around for someone to introduce himself to.

He was looking for the lead detective, but he'd learned the hard way over the years not to just assume it was the 50-something white guy in a trench coat. Especially since that guy was holding the clipboard with the major incident log, the sign-in sheet for everyone who entered or exited the crime scene. Not exactly a Top Dog assignment. But one that could prove useful to Brunelle nonetheless. As he signed himself in—'*D. Brunelle, King Co Pros Ofc*'—he scanned the entries above his.

He nodded thanks to the clipboard holder, then ducked under the crime scene tape and called out, "Detective Emory?" The entry for '*Det. C. Emory, BPD*' had been at the very top of the log.

His decision not to stereotype the lead detective appeared even smarter as the 30-something African American woman inspecting the windshield of the Audi looked up at him. "I'm Emory."

The follow-up question, 'Who are you?' was left implied.

Brunelle was used to being recognized as a prosecutor. During the day he wore a suit, and any more in Seattle the only people who wore suits were attorneys. Even the bankers were sporting khakis and open-collar shirts. But he'd been called out of bed—his turn as the on-call homicide prosecutor—and rather than show up in jeans and a college sweatshirt to meet up with some Seattle P.D. detective he'd known for years, Brunelle was wearing the same jeans and purple 'W' sweatshirt to contact cops he'd never met before.

He did homicides. And Bellevue didn't do homicides.

"I'm Dave Brunelle." He extended his hand to Det. Emory. "King County Prosecutor's Office."

Emory visibly relaxed. He wasn't just some kook, or a reporter, or both. She shook his hand warmly. "Casey," she offered her first name. She was tall, with a medium complexion, loose black curls that fell to her shoulders, and bright, dazzling eyes. "Nice to meet you, Dave."

Brunelle nodded toward the crime scene behind her. "So, you're one of the homicide detectives?" he inquired.

Emory shrugged, following his gaze. "Not exactly. I'm in

violent crimes. We don't have a specific homicide unit. This kind of stuff doesn't happen in Bellevue."

"Right," Brunelle accepted the explanation without comment.

"What about you?" Emory continued the icebreaker. "Do you do other violent crimes?"

Brunelle shook his head. "No. Just homicides."

"Sounds uplifting," Emory joked.

Brunelle smiled weakly. "It has its moments." He pointed to the Audi. "So what do we have here?"

Emory turned and led him to the center of the carnage—and even that was politely controlled to within just a few feet of the luxury automobile parked beneath the high-end shops and million-dollar condominiums. The Minotaur looked less menacing with his arm hanging out the open car door and parts of his brain stuck to the inside of the windshield.

"What do you think?" Emory asked him as Brunelle surveyed the scene.

"I think," he replied after a moment, "he's dead."

Emory cocked her head. "Really? Wow. I'm so glad you came."

"Happy to help," Brunelle grinned to her, but then returned to his appraisal of the victim. "He was seated when he was shot from behind," he observed aloud. "There's one bullet impact on the windshield, but..." He craned his neck to look at the back of the victim's head—or what was left of it—laying on his right shoulder. "There's a lot of blood and it's dark in here. I can't quite tell if there was more than one shot."

"There were two shots," came a voice from behind them.

Brunelle stood up straight to see the speaker. He was a frail-looking older man, with a shock of white hair and a skeletal frame not at all hidden under a light blue windbreaker.

"Dr. Kaladi," Brunelle knew. He was one of the assistant medical examiners Brunelle had met over the years. "They still sending you out on these?"

Kaladi shrugged and offered a strong smile of large, yellow teeth. "I'm not dead yet," he chuckled at his own joke. Medical examiner humor. "And I live on the Eastside. Redmond, home of Microsoft, Nintendo, and the Kaladi family. Besides, I don't sleep much any more at my age, so I might as well be useful."

Brunelle acknowledged the explanation with a nod. "So, two shots?" Back to business.

"Yep." Kaladi stepped around Brunelle to the body and gingerly tipped the victim's head forward. He pointed at the base of the man's skull, "Here," then higher up, dead center, so to speak, "and here."

When Brunelle didn't say anything, Kaladi added, "It's hard to see with the blood and stippling, but I was able to put my finger in each of them. There are definitely two entrance wounds."

Brunelle looked again at the windshield. "Only one exit wound, though?"

"Correct," Kaladi confirmed. "It looks like the lower shot exited just below his nose, taking some teeth with it. The higher shot likely couldn't exit the skull and ricocheted through the poor man's brain until it came to rest inside. Pretty typical, actually. But I'll confirm at the autopsy."

Brunelle glanced again at the windshield then back at the victim and, more so, the position of the driver's seat. "The neck shot was first, I think. Trajectory makes sense."

Kaladi nodded. "Agreed. The second shot likely occurred after he slumped forward. Harder to determine because there's no secondary bullet impact, but I might be able to tell from the angle of the beveling of the skull." He pointed again at the bullet wound obscured by the blood and matted hair on the back of the man's skull. "But look at that burning of the flesh. It was a contact wound. Whoever did this came up from behind and executed this man. He never had a chance."

"Wow," Emory finally jumped into the conversation. "I'm glad you two are here."

Brunelle smiled. "Oh, me too. Nothing like a night with another nameless murder victim."

"Ah, see," Emory smiled herself, raising a finger in the air. "Now that's where local law enforcement has its value too. We may not have a lot of murders in Bellevue, but we still have plenty of crime. And our victim here was well-known to B.P.D. Jerry Jenkins. Drug addict, thief, vandal, and all-around irritant. We've all arrested him at least once for something. Shoplifting, trespassing, unlawful bus conduct."

Brunelle raised an eyebrow. "Unlawful bus conduct?"

"It's a misdemeanor to smoke at the transit center," Emory explained.

"It is?"

Emory nodded. "Yep."

"That's stupid," Brunelle opined.

"Probably," Emory laughed. "But it lets us contact people at the transit center and check for warrants. Jerry always had a warrant or two out." She looked at the victim, her expression softening a bit from its heretofore professional detachment. "But never for anything serious. He was a misdemeanor guy. Substance abuse and mild mental illness. But nothing violent. Nothing that would get him executed."

"And nothing that would get him in an Audi A4," Brunelle guessed. "So maybe there was more to good ol' Jerry than you knew."

Emory shrugged. "Maybe. But we get to know some of these guys pretty well. The car is likely stolen, so he could trade it for drugs maybe."

"You think it was a drug rip?" Brunelle posited.

"Maybe," Emory shrugged. "I just don't know who else would walk up to Jerry and shoot him in the back of the head for no apparent reason."

Another sudden voice from behind them. "We have the shooter on video, Detective Emory," called out one of the uniformed patrol officers, gesturing excitedly toward the other end of the garage. "The security guy finally got here and was able to pull it up."

"Who was it?" Emory asked. "Do we have an I.D.?"

"Oh yeah," the officer answered, wide-eyed. "You can see his face clear as day. And you're not gonna freaking believe who it was."

CHAPTER 2

Brunelle expected the 'security office' to be a concrete bunker shoved into the corner of the garage, with a grainy, black-and-white monitor and a pimple-faced twenty-year-old in an ill-fitting polyester uniform. Instead, an elevator ride to a secure floor opened onto a massive, high-tech control room, with a dozen flat-screen monitors, a team of sharply dressed security personnel, and that 50-something white guy who actually was in charge.

"Hi, there." The man reached out and grabbed Brunelle's hand almost before Brunelle could extend it. "I'm Ken Tanner, Head of Security for Lincoln Properties. Great to meet you."

Ken Tanner was tall, at least 6'4", and solid, probably pushing 300 lbs., with white hair, large glasses, and a big meaty hand that swallowed Brunelle's as they shook.

"Nice to meet you too, Mr. Tanner," Brunelle answered.

"Please. Call me Ken," he instructed,

Brunelle didn't argue. He just gave his own name in return and suggested 'Ken' call him 'Dave.'

Emory had come along too. "Officer Sanders said you have the shooter on video?" she asked.

Emory seemed perfectly comfortable in Lincoln Properties' underground nerve center. Brunelle felt like he'd been transported to NATO High Command. If NATO's main goal was nabbing shoplifters and car prowlers, that is. Apparently the awe showed on his face.

"Pretty impressive, isn't it?" Tanner asked him with a slap to the back. "Come on. I'll show you on our way to the playback room."

He led the way through the command center, gesturing as he spoke. "We have cameras on every floor of every building we own. This one, the other three office towers, and of course, the mall. Most floors have multiple cameras, catching everyone coming or going from at least two angles. We have first-line security staff who are never more than two minutes away from an incident anywhere on the four blocks we own. Our team would be the fifth largest police force in Washington, if we weren't private. And our tech is state of the art. Facial recognition, infrared, you name it."

Brunelle was amazed. "Why would you need facial recognition software?" he asked. "Terrorists?"

"No," Tanner laughed. "Shoplifters. If you shoplift at one of our tenant's stores, we trespass you from all of our properties. If you come back, we'll know it."

"And two minutes later, you'll be showing them the door," Brunelle surmised.

"Almost." Another laugh from Tanner. "In two minutes, our security will have you in flex-cuffs and detain you until the cops arrive. We prosecute all shoplifters, all trespassers, everyone."

Well, technically, the prosecutor does that, Brunelle thought. But he understood the sentiment.

"Here we are," Tanner announced as they reached an impressive-looking brushed steel door about halfway down a long hallway that probably led to even more impressive-looking brushed steel doors. "The playback room."

Tanner opened the door with a clunk and flourish and motioned Brunelle and Emory inside. Brunelle had expected more flat screen monitors. Maybe a cheese tray. What he found was a miniature movie theater.

"Grab a seat," Tanner instructed. "I'll pull up the clip." And he headed behind them to what Brunelle could only assume was the projector room.

He and Emory did as they were told, Brunelle still in awe of his surroundings, Emory nonplussed. The movie seats were overstuffed leather, with drink holders.

Before Brunelle could even think of a comment to make, the wall-sized screen in front of them flickered for a moment, then they were presented with a frozen image of the Audi parked in the same stall Brunelle had found it in when he arrived. Various digits and symbols occupied the edges of the image, denoting date, time, and other similar information.

"Okay, here we go!" Tanner called out from behind them and the video started. Brunelle leaned forward and watched the action unfold.

At first, there was nothing. Just a car sitting by itself at the far end of the garage. The camera was several hundred feet away, so they couldn't really see the driver, but they hadn't come to do that. Emory already had identified the victim, and Kaladi would confirm via dental records. They'd come to I.D. the shooter. The car sat motionless, but the seconds on the time-counter sped forward. After several more seconds of nothing, and just before Brunelle was going to suggest Tanner fast forward the video, a figure walked into the frame. He was also a hundred feet or more from the camera, but he was clearly visible. Dark pants and a hoodie pulled up over his head. His hand at the low ready holding what was unmistakably a handgun.

Brunelle considered mentioning that he couldn't see the guy's face, but decided to wait for the full clip before complaining. The figure lined himself up to approach the Audi from directly behind the driver's side—exactly where someone sitting in the driver's seat wouldn't see him coming. He walked straight up to the car, stopping just before the driver's side window, then he raised the firearm and fired. There was no sound, but the muzzle flash was clearly visible. The figure then opened the car door and reached inside to fire again—point blank at the back of the victim's head. Just like Kaladi had surmised.

Again, there was no sound, just a flash of light from within the vehicle. The figure pulled his arm back to his side and walked briskly away. No effort to interact with the victim or the vehicle in any way. It wasn't a foiled car-jacking, or a drug deal gone wrong. It wasn't anything other than an execution. Again, just as they'd deduced from the scene three floors above them. The only surprise came when the figure suddenly turned and walked back off screen at the same place he'd appeared, all without his face ever being seen.

"I thought you said you identified the shooter?" Brunelle called out, assuming Tanner could hear him from wherever he'd disappeared to. "There's no way we I.D. him from that, even with your facial recognition stuff. His face can't be more than a few pixels across, and it was shaded by his hoodie."

"Way ahead of you, Dave," Tanner's voice responded in the darkness. "This was just to show you we had the right guy. Date, time, height, location, clothing. That's all going to match this second clip. I told you, we have at least two cameras on every floor. We have five on this one. A garage full of luxury cars attracts a lot of would-be car prowlers."

Brunelle supposed that made sense.

The screen flashed to a new image. It was a tight shot of the elevator bay, 'P4' painted in six-foot-high orange letters. When the doors opened, out walked the figure they'd seen on the first clip, only he filled up the entire center of the screen. It was definitely the same guy: same hoodie, same arm held to his side, same handgun not at all hidden from view. As he stepped out of the elevator, he looked quickly in either direction, with Tanner pausing the video as the man turned back to his right. Even with the hoodie up, there was a perfect view of his face.

Brunelle thought he noticed Emory gasp as he asked, "Did your software recognize him from a previous shoplift?"

"You don't recognize him?" Emory asked.

As Brunelle turned to answer, Tanner reappeared in the room. "No need for facial recognition to identify this man, Dave."

Brunelle looked again at the face enlarged on the screen in front of him. He definitely didn't recognize the man. He just looked like another middle-aged white guy in a hoodie. In an abandoned parking garage. Carrying a gun.

"Who is he?" Brunelle asked.

"That," Tanner said, stepping to the screen and pointing at the face, "is none other than Neil Rappaport."

Brunelle waited for a moment for the name to ring a bell. Nothing. "Who?"

"Neil Rappaport?" Emory repeated in disbelief. "Founder of RapTech? The biggest tech start-up in the last ten years? He's a gazillionaire. He bought two lots on Lake Washington so he'd have enough space to park both of his yachts."

Ring.

"Oh," Brunelle said simply. "Neil Rappaport. *Co*-founder of

RapTech," he corrected.

"You know him?" Emory confirmed.

"Not exactly," Brunelle answered grimly. "But I know his wife."

CHAPTER 3

"Long story," was all Brunelle would say in response to the obvious question.

Instead, he pushed the conversation back onto them. "Are you sure about the I.D.?"

"Absolutely," Tanner answered.

"Yes," Emory agreed. "That's definitely Rappaport."

"Good," Brunelle answered. Then he put them to task. "Ken, we'll need copies of these videos. In fact, save everything from every camera in this building. We'll want to go through it all eventually."

He turned to Emory. "You know where Rappaport lives?"

"Oh, yeah," she laughed. "It's a freaking compound. Gated entry, the whole bit."

"Go get him,"" Brunelle instructed. "My guess is, a guy like that probably has a team of lawyers on his payroll. None of them knows shit about criminal, but even they will know you need a warrant if he doesn't let you in. He just shot somebody in the back of the head. He's not opening his gate for you. Get ahold of the on-call judge and get the arrest warrant in advance. Then it won't matter if he opens the gate or not. You can kick it in."

"Good idea," Emory agreed. "But that'll take some time. What are you going to do? Look up that wife of his you claim you know?"

Brunelle shook his head. "No. He tapped on the 'W' on his chest. "I'm gonna look up my old college roommate."

* * *

Some gardens have even nicer gardens within.

It didn't take much for Brunelle to track down his old college roommate, Paul Cross. He had a full name and actually remembered Paul's birthday was in December, so it was just a matter of searching the state's court database. Not everybody had their DNA uploaded to the nationwide CODIS system after getting convicted of a violent (or nonviolent, in some states) felony, but almost everybody got a speeding ticket now and then. Or, in Paul's case, a seatbelt violation. No crimes, though. That was nice. It was good to be reminded that not everyone in the world was a criminal, or had a job supported by them. Some people just mail in their tickets with full payment and keep their address current with the Department of Licensing. Paul didn't live in Bellevue, though. He lived next door, in the even more affluent, more exclusive suburb of Clyde Hill. The garden's garden.

Unlike Neil Rappaport's compound, Paul Cross had no security gate. In fact, none of the residences on that particular row of mansions had gates. They were so far imbedded in their own affluence, they didn't need them. The opposite of the iron bars on the pawn shops and convenience stores in the bad part of town. The poor part of town. Brunelle hesitated for a moment, wrestling aside the natural instinct to compare his friend's success with his own—an unfavorable comparison, to be sure—then turned down the long, manicured drive to the manse within.

The home wasn't as ostentatious as Brunelle had anticipated. There was the obligatory circle drive in front, but otherwise, the house itself just seemed a little larger, a little nicer, a little fancier than a typical suburban Tudor. Brunelle estimated six bedrooms, maybe seven. Not huge, although still considerably larger than his own two-bedroom condo. The creamy white façade was lit from below by sunken floodlights, even at that late hour, making the residence seem more like a hotel, ready to welcome guests at any hour.

But it wasn't a hotel and Brunelle wasn't a weary traveler. His arrival was likely to surprise the occupants.

Brunelle parked in the drive and ascended the stone steps. It took a moment to locate the doorbell imbedded in the combination security panel and two-way speaker. He wondered how many times he might have to press it before someone woke up enough to answer the door. He also wondered if that person might end up being a servant of some sort. Did rich people have servants any more?

The answers were: one time; and no, apparently not.

Just as Brunelle reached out to press the doorbell a second time, the front door opened and there stood Paul Cross, twenty-some years older, but unmistakably the same man Brunelle had roomed with at the University of Washington.

"Hello?" Paul started. "Can I help you?"

Apparently, he didn't recognize Brunelle. Then again, Brunelle had the advantage of knowing who they both were in advance of their reunion.

"Paul, it's me," he said. "Dave. Dave Brunelle."

Paul narrowed his eyes and cocked his head slightly. "Dave? Holy crap, it is you!" He reached out and clapped Brunelle on the shoulders. "What the hell are you doing here?"

"I'm here on business, Paul," Brunelle said grimly. "I'm a prosecutor with the King County Prosecutor's Office now."

Paul's hands recoiled. "Oh shit, Dave. Are you here to bust me?"

Brunelle smiled slightly at what he assumed was a joke. "No, Paul. Nothing like that. It's about Vickie."

Paul's eyebrows shot up. "Vickie?" he repeated. "Oh, crap."

He glanced past Brunelle, then reached out for his shoulder again. "Come on in, Dave. Let's talk inside."

Brunelle had no trouble agreeing. He stepped out of the dark of the night into the brightly lit foyer of Paul Cross's luxurious home. If Brunelle hadn't known it was well past midnight, he would have thought it was the middle of the day. The house was completely lit up and Brunelle noticed Paul was still in his street clothes—no pajamas or robe.

"I'm sorry to bother you like this," Brunelle said as Paul led them through the marble-floored entryway into a large, open-floor-plan kitchen area. There was a view of Lake Washington out a picture window, Seattle's nighttime skyline visible across the water. "Something's happened. Something big, I need to talk to your sister. I thought maybe you could get ahold of her for me."

Paul grabbed a bourbon bottle from the counter and started pouring two drinks. "I should have known, Dave. After all this time, you didn't come to see me. You came to see Vickie." He handed Brunelle his glass. "Just like old times."

Brunelle laughed a little, in spite of himself. "Not exactly like old times," he insisted. "I'm not asking you to introduce me to your hot little sister."

"Paul?" A woman's voice came from a darkened hallway off the kitchen. "Is everything okay?"

Victoria Cross—Victoria *Rappaport*—stepped into the lights

of the kitchen. And Brunelle stepped twenty years into the past. He was in college again. Seeing his roommate's sister for the first time again. His heart racing again.

"Dave?" she said when she saw him, her expression at least as surprised as Brunelle knew his own was. "David Brunelle?"

She had the same pale blue eyes. The same long, black curls. The same curves hiding, but discernable, under her white, terrycloth robe.

"Vickie," Brunelle replied after he caught his breath. "I— I didn't— That is... Wow, it's good to see you again."

Vickie took a moment to confirm the situation. "Wow. Dave Brunelle. After all this time." She tightened her robe, then tried smoothing her hair back. "Crap. I look terrible. It's like three a.m. What are you doing here? What...? Why...? Holy crap. David fucking Brunelle. Wow."

Brunelle agreed. "Yeah. It's been a long time. I—" He looked at Paul and back to his sister. "I'm sorry. I didn't know you'd be here."

"Dave's a prosecutor now, Vic," Paul offered. "He says you're in trouble."

"No," Brunelle immediately interjected. "It's not about you, Vickie." He paused. "It's about Neil."

Vickie's countenance hardened. She crossed her arms. "What about him?"

Brunelle paused. He hadn't expected to talk to Vickie that soon, and certainly not in person. But opportunities were meant to be taken. He could start building his case against Rappaport right then. His interest in Vickie was purely professional. Really.

"Was Neil engaged in anything shady?" Brunelle asked. "Anything that might lead him to be alone, late at night, in a parking garage, with a known thief and drug addict?"

Vickie didn't respond immediately. Her expression looked confused. Almost hurt.

"I'm sorry, Vickie," Brunelle said. "I know he's your husband."

That elicited the immediate response. "No." She raised a hand for emphasis. "Actually, he's not. He divorced me. It became final just last Friday."

Brunelle's jaw dropped. "What? Why?" Then, after another moment with Victoria Cross—*not* Victoria Rappaport—he expressed his honest thought. "Is he crazy?"

"Actually," Paul put in, "we were wondering the same thing."

Brunelle turned to his old roommate.

"He did kind of go nuts," Paul explained. "He's been trying to get me out of the company for months. First, he offered to buy me out. When I blew him off, he sued, claiming I was no longer capable of running the company. He used the fact that I wouldn't sell to him as evidence that I didn't have the company's best interest at heart. The case got thrown out almost as fast as he filed it, of course. Then he suddenly filed for divorce. He served Vickie with the papers, then called me and said he'd drop the divorce if I sold out to him."

"He told me the same thing," Vickie added. "But no. Filing for divorce is not a negotiating tactic. You don't walk back from that. Neil actually seemed surprised when I told him that, but then he said, fine. But he warned me not to drag it out. If I agreed to let it take effect at the end of the mandatory ninety-day waiting period, he'd give me ten thousand a month support and agree to only seeing the kids two weekends a month. But if I took it past the ninety days, he'd fight to pay the minimum and demand fifty-fifty joint custody of the kids."

Brunelle shook his head.

Vickie shrugged. "It was a no-brainer. I agreed to the ninety-day deal. That ended on Friday. The lawyers filed the papers, and I got an email from my lawyer that afternoon with the signed dissolution decree. I was officially divorced."

"Single again," Brunelle thought aloud.

Vickie laughed lightly. "Yeah. Wow. Nice to see you haven't changed after all these years, Dave."

Brunelle tried to regain an air of professionalism. "So, ten thousand a month and primary custody of the kids?"

"Yep." Vickie nodded. "Like I said, easy decision. He'd been distant and neglectful for a long time anyway. I mean, don't get me wrong, I was shocked. But then I wasn't. And I have to do what's best for my kids."

"How many kids?" Brunelle tried to sound casual. Or professional. Or something.

Vickie smiled. "Two. Neil Junior is eight and Emily is four."

Brunelle didn't know what his response to that should be. Before he could say something stupid, little Emily toddled into the light, rubbing her eyes.

"Mommy?" she squeaked. "Is that Daddy?"

"Crap," Vickie said as she turned and pulled her daughter against her hip. "No, honey. It's just an old friend."

She picked the girl up and she buried her sleepy face into her mother's neck.

"I better get her back to bed," Vickie said. Then she pointed at Brunelle. "Don't leave."

"Of course not," Brunelle answered.

"Please," Vickie continued. "Don't leave without saying goodbye. Not again."

Brunelle swallowed hard. He nodded. "Okay."

Then he watched as Vickie disappeared into the hallway.

"Wow," Paul commented after a moment. "I'd forgotten how intense you two were."

"Yeah," Brunelle answered absently, still looking after Vickie. *The hottest flames burn the fastest,* he thought.

His phone rang then and shook him from his memories. He pulled it from his pocket and turned to look out the window as he answered. "Brunelle."

It was Emory. "We're at Rappaport's."

That was quick, Brunelle thought. "Is there a problem?"

"No," Emory answered. "We had the warrant in hand, but we didn't need it. He let us in and was completely cooperative. Almost passive. He's sitting in his living room with two patrol guys sitting on him. That's why I'm calling."

"Did he say anything?"

"No, he lawyered up," Emory reported. "The only statement he made was, when we told him we wanted to talk to him about the murder of Jerry Jenkins, he said, 'I don't know who that is.'"

There was a pause as Brunelle considered the information.

"So, no confession," Emory confirmed. All we have is the video. What do you want me to do?"

Brunelle turned and looked again at the darkened hallway where Vickie had disappeared with her child.

"That's enough," he told Emory. "It'll have to be. Arrest him."

He hung up and returned the phone to his pocket. Then he looked at Paul. "I have to go."

Paul stood up from his seat at the kitchen table. "What's going on, Dave? Why are you here? What's happening with Neil?"

Brunelle set his mouth to a hard line. "I'm charging him with murder."

CHAPTER 4

There's no such thing as bad publicity.

Unless you're a prosecutor and the ethical rules bar you from commenting on pending cases.

The only thing worse than Brunelle facing a cadre of reporters after the arrest of one of Seattle's biggest tech giants was Brunelle's boss being accosted by the same cadre without knowing Neil Rappaport had been arrested for murder.

Brunelle got into the office early. Matt Duncan, his boss and the elected District Attorney for King County, had gotten in even earlier.

Brunelle walked past the still-empty desk of Duncan's administrative assistant and knocked on Duncan's open door.

The boss looked up. He managed to both smile and then frown in the same split second. "Oh, crap, Dave. What happened?"

Brunelle dropped his arms. "Really? Can't a loyal employee—and dare I say, friend?—stop by his boss's office to wish him a good morning?"

Duncan smiled but shook his head. "No. Not you." He looked at his watch. "Not this early. Something happened last night.

Somebody's dead and your shit is about to hit my fan."

"I'm hurt," Brunelle offered.

"And I'm right," Duncan asserted.

Brunelle shrugged. "Well, yeah."

Duncan laughed and motioned for Brunelle to come inside. "What happened?" he repeated.

Brunelle took a seat across from Duncan's desk "Do you know who Neil Rappaport is?"

Duncan thought for a moment. He shook his head. "No. Should I?"

Brunelle shrugged again. "I don't know. Probably. He's some rich and famous tech guy."

"Ah," Duncan tipped his head back. "The tech industry. I remember when this town used to build airplanes."

"We still build airplanes," Brunelle pointed out.

Duncan conceded the point with a grunt. "I also remember when, if you wanted to get rich, you went to law school or medical school."

Brunelle laughed at that. "Yeah, we're both old enough to remember that lie. But the reward of public service can't be reduced to mere dollars."

"I can see why you do so well in front of juries," Duncan smiled. "I almost believed that."

Brunelle nodded his head in thanks. He always enjoyed his conversations with Duncan. They made the world slow down, mercifully, even if only temporarily. But there was business to get to. "Rappaport was arrested last night. I'm charging him with Murder One. The arraignment will be at one-thirty. And your phone is about to blow up."

Duncan's smile faded. "Okay, then. Thanks for the warning. So, who did he kill? A business rival? A neighbor over a property dispute? A high-end call girl? I assume it's something glitzy and salacious."

"A drug addict and petty thief," Brunelle answered. "Shot him execution-style in an underground parking garage in Bellevue last night."

Duncan frowned. "Why in the world would he do that?"

"No idea," Brunelle answered. "But it's on videotape. Clear as day.

"The jury is going to want a motive," Duncan observed.

"So is the media," Brunelle added. "You handle them and I'll handle the jury."

"What do you want me to tell them?" Duncan asked. "That there's no apparent motive?"

Brunelle grimaced. "How about: The investigation is ongoing?"

"Okay," Duncan nodded. "But you'll have to come up with something better for the jurors. Investigations are supposed to be complete before the trial."

"I know," Brunelle replied. "I will. Unless I can't."

Duncan considered for a moment. "So who do you want as your second chair?"

Brunelle shifted in his seat. "Well, actually, I was thinking I would just handle this on my own."

Duncan raised an eyebrow. "You don't want co-counsel?"

"I don't need one," Brunelle responded. "It's on videotape. The I.D. is solid. Rappaport did it. It won't take two prosecutors to press play on the projector."

Duncan didn't seem convinced. But he did seem willing to trust Brunelle. "All right, Dave. But you'll keep me posted as the case falls apart, right?"

Brunelle stood up and smiled. "I always do."

CHAPTER 5

Shit.

Brunelle stepped off the courthouse elevator and into a throng of reporters and cameramen. The entrance to the arraignment court was on the other side of the media mob. He knew most of the local guys, and once they saw him, he'd be in the middle of a 'Comment, please' feeding frenzy. The last thing he wanted to do was comment on the case. He'd learned that lesson a long time ago. There were ethical bars to a prosecutor commenting on a pending case. And besides, what was he going to say when they asked, 'Why did he do it?'

He looked for a way around the paparazzi. Surprisingly, he found it.

"Dave," Detective Emory whispered from the other end of the hallway. She was holding open a secure door to a back hallway. "This way."

Brunelle didn't have to be asked twice. He hurried away from the crowd and followed Emory into the secure holding area behind the courtrooms on the top floor of the courthouse, used to transport the in-custody defendants between the jail and the courtroom.

"What are you doing here?" he asked as the door clunked shut behind them. "Not that I'm not glad to see you."

Emory smiled. "Nice to see you too, Dave. And are you kidding? There's no way I'm going to miss the arraignment on this case. We don't get a lot of murder cases over in Bellevue, and this one is crazy. I'm coming to all the court hearings."

Brunelle liked the sound of that. It was always nice to have an ally. But he didn't say so.

"And I've got some exciting news," she added. "Something I thought you'd want to know before you did the arraignment."

Brunelle liked the sound of that. "What?"

"The forensics guys pulled a fingerprint off the elevator, on the 'close door' button," she said. "It's Rappaport's. The fingerprint tech called me this morning."

Brunelle smiled. "That's awesome."

"I know, right?" Emory said. "Of course, he'll say he pressed it some other time he was in the elevator."

"That would only work if no one else ever pressed that button afterward," Brunelle responded, already seeing that defense. "Possible, but not reasonable."

Emory smiled. "Glad that lifted your spirits," she said.

Brunelle frowned slightly. "My spirits are fine," he assured.

"Well, you didn't look happy to fight through that crowd of reporters," Emory observed, gesturing behind them.

"Well, that's true," he admitted. "Am I that easy to read?"

The corridor was all cement, with an unfinished concrete floor and cinderblock walls, all painted a lovely shade of medium gray. Their shoes clacked as they made their way toward the holding cell where the day's defendants were being watched by uniformed corrections officers until it was their turn to be arraigned.

"It's my job to read people," Emory explained with a shrug.

"Oh, yeah?" Brunelle responded. They'd reached the entrance to the courtroom, right next to the holding cell. "Can you read me right now?"

Emory narrowed her eyes for a moment, then tried, "You're nervous. Or more anxious really." She paused. "And irritated. Or irritable, anyway."

Brunelle tried to keep a poker face. He didn't like being readable. He was irritated, at being anxious.

"Are you anxious about the arraignment?" Emory followed up, with a tip of her head toward the courtroom on the other side of the door they were standing in front of.

Brunelle scoffed. "I'm not anxious about an arraignment." That much was true. Arraignments were about as perfunctory as it could get. It was the first hearing—the very beginning of a long road. He was anxious about being able to prove the case at the end of it all. "I'm not anxious at all," he insisted. "And not irritable either. Looks like you need to work on your people-reading skills."

Emory crossed her arms and smiled. "Sure."

Brunelle looked over Emory's shoulder at the holding tank for the inmates about to be arraigned. He spotted Rappaport—or at least it looked like the man from the video—sitting against the far wall, dressed in the red inmate scrubs of the King County Jail and not engaging with the other defendants. He seemed to sense Brunelle's gaze and looked up. They locked eyes for a second and then Rappaport looked away. He didn't know who Brunelle was. Not yet.

"Let's head in," Brunelle suggested. "Maybe I can get us to the front of the line."

Rappaport wasn't the only one for an arraignment. Everyone

who'd committed a felony in King County the previous night was also scheduled to be arraigned. Burglars, drug dealers, aggravated assaulters. But everyone was there for the murderer. The judge would probably appreciate getting him done first, and draining the gallery of the media presence. Emory nodded to the corrections officer behind the control room glass, and the door unlocked with a clunk. Emory entered first and took a standing spot in a back corner of the secure area separated from the gallery by yet another door and floor to ceiling bulletproof glass. Brunelle walked up to the young prosecutor stationed at the bar below the still empty judge's bench.

"Hey there," Brunelle greeted the young man. "Any chance I could go first? I've got the Rappaport arraignment."

The young prosecutor snapped to attention. "Hello, Mr. Brunelle," he replied. Brunelle felt a little bad that he didn't know the young man's name as well, but it was a big office. Every prosecutor started in the misdemeanor division, then moved on to felonies after a few years. One of the first felony assignments was this young man's lot: doing just arraignments, one after another, all day, every day. He hadn't had a chance to make a name for himself yet. Brunelle had. "Of course, Mr. Brunelle. I assumed you'd want to go first, what with all the cameras and all."

Brunelle glanced again at the gallery. He wondered if there was anyone in there who didn't work for a news organization. Brunelle had his file with the charging documents. The State was ready.

"Has the defense attorney checked in with you yet?" Brunelle asked. It was the only other thing they'd need before they could do the arraignment. He wondered if it would just be the stand-in public defender until Rappaport could make arrangements to hire private counsel. No way he'd qualify for the public defender, but no one got arraigned without at least standby counsel at their side.

"Yes, sir," the prosecutor said. He pointed to the far counsel table. "They're right over there."

They?

Brunelle turned to see three sharply dressed attorneys huddled, whispering, and generally looking out of place in the otherwise threadbare world of government attorneys. There was a very tall older man with white hair and a neatly trimmed white beard; a shorter, heavyset man with thick black hair and a ruddy complexion; and a woman, her height between the two men, with jaw-length brown hair and a thin mouth. None of them looked like they enjoyed themselves very much. And Brunelle didn't recognize any of them.

He walked over and extended a hand somewhere in the middle of all three of them. "Hi. I'm Dave Brunelle. I'm the prosecutor on the Rappaport case."

The attorneys stopped their whispering and opened their huddle enough to look at him. But no one took his hand. "Harold Voegel," the tall man replied. Then he nodded to his two companions. "Lisa Walker and Eric Khachaturian. We represent Mr. Rappaport."

Brunelle pulled his hand back. "Nice to meet you," he lied. Again, he didn't recognize any of them, and he knew most of the defense attorneys in town, especially the ones who handled murders. He supposed these might be Rappaport's corporate attorneys, available on short notice.

"Are you appearing just for the arraignment?" Brunelle asked.

"Uh, no," Lisa Walker replied with a smug chuckle. "We'll be representing Mr. Rappaport all the way from the arraignment through the dismissal of charges."

Brunelle grimaced. Already trash-talking. "Great." He ignored the barb. "Are you ready to proceed then? I can get us to go first, if you're ready."

"We were ready an hour after Mr. Rappaport was arrested," Eric Khachaturian replied.

Another pained smile. Another "Great." And Brunelle returned to the prosecutor's place at the bar. He didn't bother offering his hand again. "We're ready whenever the judge is," he informed his younger colleague, as well as the bailiff who was seated between where the attorneys stood and the judge sat. A few short minutes later, the judge took the bench and Brunelle called the case.

"The first matter that's ready, Your Honor," he announced, "is the State of Washington versus Neil Rappaport."

A murmur rippled through the gallery and the corrections officer opened the door to the holding cell. "Rappaport!" he called out. A few seconds later, Rappaport waddled out into the courtroom, his movement retarded by the chains on his feet and waist, restricting his hands to no more than a few inches from his body. He took a position at the bar, a few feet away from Brunelle and flanked by his team of attorneys.

Arraignments had two purposes: First, to advise the defendant of the charges against him; and second, to set a bail amount. The first part was easy. The judge read the charges and the defense attorney entered a plea of 'Not Guilty.' The real battle was in what bail the court might set. But that wasn't going to be an issue either. Not with the founder of RapTech standing before the tribunal.

After accepting the not guilty plea, the judge turned to look down at Brunelle. "What is the State's position regarding conditions of release?"

Brunelle nodded. Standard bail for Murder One was a million dollars, maybe two million if there really was a reason to suspect the defendant might flee or go after the witnesses. But a million-dollar bail could be posted by paying a bail company $100,000—ten percent of the bail amount. Or by liquidating probably five percent of his RapTech stock, which his lawyers had probably done within two hours of Rappaport being arrested.

"The State would ask the Court to hold Mr. Rappaport without bail, Your Honor," Brunelle said. "We expect he would be able to post any dollar amount the Court might set, and we don't believe a defendant's custody status should depend on how wealthy he or she is."

The judge raised his eyebrows at Brunelle. He was one of the older judges, with thinning hair and a gray beard, a little on the scruffy side. In fact, he'd already announced he was retiring rather than run again for reelection He'd been a judge longer than Brunelle had been a lawyer. And they both knew that a criminal defendant in Washington couldn't be held without bail pending trial unless it was a capital murder case or a third strike. This was neither. Capital murder—death penalty eligible murder—required some additional, statutorily defined aggravating factor: like killing two or more people at once, or killing a cop or judge, or committing the murder during the course of another serious crime like robbery or rape. The irony was that killing a random stranger for no reason in cold blood—the definition of a psychopath—was the murder least eligible for the death penalty.

So, it wasn't a capital case. And it wasn't a third strike either. The only thing on Rappaport's history was an unsafe lane change ticket he'd gotten dismissed on a deferral four years earlier. Which meant Brunelle's request for a no bail hold was illegal. It was also a test.

And old Judge Crosby seemed to get it.

Instead of arguing with Brunelle, he turned to the defense team. "Any response?" he asked, looking to Voegel.

Voegel hesitated. He looked at Walker, but then nodded to Khachaturian, who stepped forward to respond.

"May it please the Court," he started formally. "Eric Khachaturian appearing on behalf of the accused, Neil Rappaport. Your Honor is well aware, I'm sure, that Article One, Section Twenty, of the Washington State Constitution guarantees the right of criminal defendants to secure their presence through the posting of bail. A court may only deny bail for capital offenses and third strikes, and even then only when the Court determines that such a no bail hold is required for the safety of the community. Mr. Rappaport is not charged with capital murder nor is he facing a third strike. The prosecutor's request is unlawful."

Brunelle frowned slightly. So Khachaturian knew some criminal law. At least for a bail hearing.

Voegel jumped in. "We would ask the Court to sanction Mr. Brunelle for attempting to violate our client's constitutional rights, Your Honor. His request was flagrant and ill-intentioned."

And Voegel was a civil litigator, Brunelle surmised. They were always asking for the other side to get sanctioned. It was a negotiating tactic in the game of high-stakes corporate lawsuits. But criminal law wasn't a game. Or it was, but less so.

"I'm not going to impose sanctions on anyone," Judge Crosby replied dismissively. "Mr. Brunelle was trying to make a point, I believe, that persons like your client who have access to large sums of money are treated differently by the criminal justice system from accused who don't enjoy such resources. I've known Mr. Brunelle for a long time and he knows I wouldn't set an illegal bail. Your motion for sanctions is denied."

He turned again to Brunelle. "Do you want to make an actual bail recommendation?"

Brunelle shrugged. "Bail on a murder case is usually one or two million dollars, depending on the facts and the defendant's criminal history. I imagine Mr. Rappaport probably had that in his wallet when he was booked. So, I don't know, how about one billion dollars?"

It was a flippant request, unlikely to be granted, and met with predictable gasps and chuckles from the other attorneys assembled to take their turns after Rappaport was done.

"A billion dollars?" Judge Crosby repeated.

Another shrug. "It might actually hold him pending trial," Brunelle offered. "Otherwise, he could be on a private plane to Brazil within the hour."

The judge nodded slightly, at that last point anyway. He looked again to Khachaturian. "I assume you think bail should be less than one billion dollars?"

The defense attorney stood up straight and tugged at his lapels. "I certainly do, Your Honor. And I must say, I'm concerned by how cavalierly Mr. Brunelle is approaching this issue. My client is an American citizen and successful businessman. He is presumed innocent. The issues surrounding his continued detention and the use of his hard-earned financial assets are not to be taken lightly."

Judge Crosby nodded impatiently. "What's your bail recommendation?"

"We would ask for the Court to release Mr. Rappaport on his personal recognizance," Khachaturian replied curtly. "Criminal Rule three-point-two mandates that a court presumes a P.R. release and—"

"I'm not releasing a murder defendant on a P.R.," Crosby

interrupted. "I'll set bail the same as I would for anyone else charged with this crime. One million dollars. Will your client be able to post that?"

Khachaturian didn't even bother confirming with his client. "Yes, Your Honor," he knew.

The judge then listed off the other conditions of release: no criminal law violations, no contact with the family of the victim, attend all future court dates. "And surrender his passport."

"Your Honor?" Khachaturian reacted. "I don't think that's necessary."

"You don't?" Judge Crosby replied. "Well, that's nice. I do. He is not to be released until his passport is turned in to the court clerk."

Khachaturian looked to Voegel and Walker. There was quick whispering, to which Rappaport added a nod, then Khachaturian looked back up at the judge. "That's fine, Your Honor. Thank you."

Crosby didn't respond. Instead he looked at the junior prosecutor assigned to his courtroom. "Next case!"

Brunelle stepped away from the bar to sign the order on conditions of release the clerk handed him. After he'd signed off he took it over to Khachaturian for his signature. Rappaport was already gone, swept back to the holding area so the next defendant in the afternoon sausage factory could get arraigned.

"Here you go," Brunelle said as he handed it to him. "You sign on page two."

Khachaturian took the form without looking at Brunelle. "I know where to sign."

Brunelle wasn't so sure. He'd never seen Khachaturian before. "Sorry. I wasn't sure if you were familiar with the forms. I haven't seen you around before. You obviously do criminal, though, right?"

Voegel—who, along with Walker, was standing behind Khachaturian—answered for him. "Mr. Khachaturian is one of the premiere criminal defense attorneys in Washington State. We have associated with him for this case."

"And you're Mr. Rappaport's personal attorneys, I take it?" Brunelle asked.

"McKenzie, Oldquist, Voegel and Rodriguez represents all of Mr. Rappaport's legal needs," Voegel replied.

Ah, a named partner. Brunelle knew he was supposed to be impressed. He wasn't. It was a corporate firm. Corporate firms didn't have trial lawyers; they had 'litigators.' And litigators did everything they could do to avoid trial. Hence, bring Khachaturian on board.

"Are you based in Seattle?" Brunelle went on. He was genuinely curious. It was always nice to meet another criminal practitioner, even one on the other side.

Khachaturian shook his head. "Bellevue. My practice is exclusively D.U.I. defense. Well, except for this case."

"D.U.I.?" Brunelle repeated. He stopped himself from adding, *'Really?'* No wonder he'd never heard of him. Brunelle hadn't tried a D.U.I. in twenty years.

"Yes," answered Khachaturian. "I enjoy the challenge of winning cases where the prosecutor has a machine that says the defendant is guilty."

"The breath test machine?" Brunelle confirmed.

Khachaturian nodded.

"Eric was voted Washington's top criminal trial attorney the last three years running by *Top Litigator* magazine," Walker put in.

Brunelle managed not to shake his head at that. His opinion was that *Top Litigator* magazine was a racket to get rich clients with no experience with the criminal justice system to hire allegedly highly rated, and unquestionably expensive lawyers. Apparently it worked.

"So, how do you win a case," Brunelle inquired, "where the State has a breath test result that says the defendant is guilty?"

He figured Khachaturian would want to brag a bit. And he wanted to get some insight into what might be coming.

"Easy," responded Khachaturian. "You suppress it. The jury expects to hear certain evidence—a number over the legal limit. When they don't, they acquit, no matter what the rest of the evidence shows."

"So how do you suppress it?" Brunelle followed up.

But Khachaturian just smiled. "You'll see."

CHAPTER 6

"You'll see" was also what Brunelle's legal assistant, Nicole Richards, said to him when he asked why he had to drive all the way out to Bellevue again to meet with the victim's family instead of having them come downtown to his office. Brunelle had rolled his eyes, but knew not to question Nicole further. He could trust her. He did trust her. So he took the map and directions she had printed out for him and headed east over Lake Washington again.

Instead of Exit 9 to the glass-and-steel garden of downtown Bellevue again, the directions had him travel two-and-a-half more miles to Exit 11B toward '156th Avenue.' He followed the directions past the two auto dealerships, the strip mall of teriyaki joints and coffee shops, and the empty retail space that had obviously once been a grocery store, until he turned north on 156th and headed toward the 'Crossroads Arms Apartments.' They were on the left-hand side, just past the Crossroads Mall with its Crossroads Cinema 16-plex, and the Crossroads Senior Living Center. He waited for traffic to clear, then turned into the parking lot of the squat, brick-façade apartment complex.

Nicole had written 'Apt 1-D' at the bottom of her directions.

Brunelle took a note to admire how pretty her handwriting was as he shut off his car and steeled himself to Meet The Family.

Meeting the family might not have been Brunelle's least favorite part of his job, but it was in the bottom three—along with hearing a jury foreperson announcing, 'Not guilty.' It wasn't that he didn't like people—which, honestly, sometimes he didn't—it was that there wasn't anything he could really do for them. But they didn't always seem to get that. Also, most of his murder victims weren't exactly choir boys living in beautiful mansions like Paul Cross. Or Victoria Cross-Rappaport.

"Just Victoria Cross again," he reminded himself with a smile as he walked across the cracked and uneven asphalt parking lot.

Apartment 1-D was on the ground floor and opened directly onto the parking lot. There was a thin sidewalk against the building that kept the cars from parking right against the building. The window was covered in heavy drapes so he couldn't see inside. Instead, he took a deep breath and knocked on the door.

There was no immediate reply, but he could hear noises inside. After a few seconds, the door opened and Brunelle was greeted by the smell of cigarette smoke and the image of a very tall, very thin man in jeans and a white tank-top.

"Yeah?" he greeted Brunelle, looking him up and down. Brunelle suddenly became very aware that he was wearing a suit and tie.

"Uh, I'm Dave Brunelle." He extended his hand. "From the King County Prosecutor's Office. I'm here to talk about Jerry. I think my assistant made an appointment with you?"

The man's cautious expression softened. "Oh, yeah." He turned back toward the interior of the apartment. "Hey, mom! That prosecutor is here! The one handling Jerry's case."

He stepped aside and motioned Brunelle inside. "Thanks for coming over. I'll get mom."

Brunelle stepped inside the small, dark apartment. The smell of cigarettes was stronger inside, mixed with other scents: food he probably wouldn't like and what was either the bathroom or unwashed laundry. He spied the sitting area and was relieved to see the couch appeared to be free of anything sticky.

"Mom," the tall man said as he reentered the living room, "this is the prosecutor, Mr. Burnell."

"Brunelle," he corrected as 'mom' entered the room.

She was on a motorized scooter, which she expertly maneuvered through the bedroom doorway and around the furniture that crowded the small living area. She was very heavyset, with long gray hair, and an oxygen tube in her nostrils. She looked at Brunelle and smiled. "Nice suit," she croaked, her gravelly voice confirming she was at least partially responsible for the cigarette smell.

Brunelle smiled. "Thanks. Nobody wears these any more."

"No, it looks nice," the woman replied kindly. "You wear it good."

Brunelle wasn't sure what to say. He didn't come to talk about his suit. "Thanks for letting me come over. I wanted to let you know what's going on with Jerry's case."

Back at the courthouse, in his office, and definitely on the news, it was the Neil Rappaport case. But right there, right then, it was the Jerry Jenkins case.

"Can I sit down?" he asked.

"Of course," the woman replied. "I'm Beverly, by the way. I'm Jerry's mom. And this is his brother, Tom."

Brunelle nodded to both of them. "Dave," he offered his first name.

"So what's happening on the case?" Beverly asked. She reached over and picked the pack of cigarettes off the coffee table between them. "Smoke?" she offered.

Brunelle declined. He didn't smoke. But he knew he was going to smell like it when he got back to the office. That suit was going straight to the dry cleaners.

"We just did the arraignment." Brunelle informed them. "The trial got set out several months, but that's normal for a murder case. Most murder cases go to trial six to twelve months after the crime. Depends on how complicated it is."

"This one isn't complicated," Beverly said. "That rich computer guy killed my boy. Simple as that. Don't know why we even need a trial."

Brunelle decided not to try to explain the Sixth Amendment right then. He understood the comment for what it was. Frustration at the loss of a loved one and the glacial pace of the criminal justice system. Luckily, he didn't need to deflect the question because Tom jumped in with a different one. One he could address.

"So, why did he do it?" Tom asked. "Jerry didn't know no rich computer guys."

Brunelle could address the question, but he couldn't answer it. "I don't actually know," he admitted. "Not yet anyway. But don't worry. I don't have to prove why he did it, just *that* he did it."

"Well, I want to know why he did it," Beverly half-yelled. "I want to know why he shot my Jerry like he was just some piece of garbage he could throw away."

Brunelle ignored the mixed metaphor. "I want to know, too," he assured her. "And I plan to figure it out. I'm just assuring you that it's not necessary to get a conviction. Even if we can't figure out why, we have it on videotape. It's him. He did it. And I'm going to do everything I can to make sure he's held responsible for it."

"Is he gonna get the death penalty?" Tom asked, his eyes understandably, but still disconcertingly, hopeful for such a result.

Brunelle shook his head. As much as he might like to bluster and promise vengeance to the victim's family, he knew better. One of the maxims of legal work—no matter what type—was to underpromise and overdeliver. Brunelle didn't have clients, but he had victims and victims' families. High expectations only led to disappointment when reality crashed into those expectations and sent them tumbling to the ground.

"No," he told them, "it's not death-eligible. You have to kill a cop or a judge or something. Or do it during a robbery. Stuff like that. But this isn't one of those cases. It's a straightforward premeditated murder."

Tom frowned. "Well, then how much time is he looking at?" he demanded.

"Twenty years minimum," Brunelle answered. "The range is twenty to twenty-five years. Plus five more for using a gun."

"Twenty-five years?" Beverly exclaimed, even as Tom threw his arms up in disgust and looked away. "For killing my baby? That's not enough!"

Brunelle had had this conversation before. More times than he could count. Every state was different. Life in prison was pretty common for Murder One, and that's how Hollywood made it look. But Washington's legislature had set the minimum penalty for premeditated murder at twenty years. He decided not to tell them that the penalty for Murder Two—intentional, but unpremeditated murder—was even more appalling: only ten years. Instead, he said the only thing that victim families ever seemed to want to hear from the prosecutor: "You're right. It's not enough."

Underpromise. Overdeliver. But still empathize.

Tom scoffed. "You can get twenty years for drugs, man. That's nothing."

Brunelle wasn't sure it was 'nothing' exactly. And the only way you were going to get twenty years for drugs was if the Feds took it, and you were running a lot of it across state lines. Still, it raised an area he had wanted to discuss.

"Speaking of that," he ventured, "do you know if Jerry was selling drugs? My cops tell me he used to do that, and I'm wondering whether maybe Rappaport was buying drugs from him. It might be a motive," he encouraged.

"My little boy didn't do drugs!" Beverly insisted.

But her surviving son waved her off. "Yes, he did, ma. We both did." He turned to Brunelle. "But we both got clean. His was meth. Mine was heroin. I'm still on methadone. I'm maybe even gonna try that suboxone. But Jerry wasn't using any more. And he wasn't selling."

Brunelle frowned. He knew enough to realize Jerry might well have been using again, and selling, without letting his family know. Especially his mom who insisted he'd always been clean, and his brother who was trying to stay clean himself. But there was nothing to be gained by having that argument then.

Instead, he tried another tack. "What about a dating relationship? Could he have been meeting Rappaport for sex?"

It was kind of a bombshell question, but Brunelle had seen a lot in his day. He guessed Tom had too.

Beverly took in a deep breath, presumably to protest her son's heterosexuality, but it caused a coughing fit and so Tom was able to step in with a calmer reaction. "I get what you're saying. Hell, I seen guys who'd do, who *did*, anything for their next fix. But Jerry never got that desperate. And like I said, he was clean. He wasn't meeting billionaires in a parking garage to trade blow jobs for drug money."

Brunelle nodded. Again, it might be something that Jerry was hiding from his family. Time to change the subject.

"So, there will be several court hearings prior to the actual trial," he explained. "Just preliminary things. You're welcome to attend, but I wouldn't recommend it—unless it's important to you to be at every single hearing. Some families want to do that. Some just want to come to the trial. It can be hard to take time off work just to watch the lawyers sign some paperwork and adjourn again after fifteen minutes."

"I want to come to every hearing," Beverly rasped. "But I need to save my strength for the trial. I want the jury to see that Jerry had a family who loved him."

"That's excellent," Brunelle agreed. "It's important for juries to see family. It reminds them the victim was a real person. Murder cases are weird like that. The one person they never get to meet is the most important person in the case: the victim. Jerry."

Lawyers could argue about whether the victim or the defendant was the most important person, but there was no argument when a prosecutor was talking with the victim's family. And it hit the mark.

"Thank you, Mr. Brunelle," Beverly said. She reached out for Brunelle's hand. He had to stand up to be able to reach her, but he did so. She squeezed his hand. "We're counting on you to get justice for Jerry."

Brunelle sighed and squeezed her hand back. "I know."

CHAPTER 7

Brunelle had really appreciated Nicole's help in arranging the meeting with the Jenkinses and making sure he found his way there. He was less appreciative a week or so later when she brought him a half-inch-thick motion on pleading paper from McKenzie, Oldquist, Voegel and Rodriguez.

"This just arrived," she announced as she dropped it on his desk with a dramatic thud. "Good luck."

Brunelle looked down at the pleading.

"'Motion to Suppress Video-recording,'" he read aloud. He looked up at Nicole. "Really?"

She shrugged. "Don't ask me. You're the lawyer."

"Yeah, but you're smarter than me," Brunelle returned.

Nicole smiled. "I won't argue with that." She nodded toward the motion. "Give it a read and let me know what you need help with."

Brunelle agreed and Nicole took her leave so he could peruse the motion.

"Suppress the video?' he asked aloud. "It's almost impossible to suppress a video or photo."

Under the evidence rules, he just needed a witness, any witness, to say it was an accurate depiction of whatever was in the image. Emory could do that. So could Tanner. Hell, even that guy with the clipboard could identify the crime scene enough to admit the video. What was Khachaturian's angle?

'You suppress it,' Brunelle remembered him saying.

"But how?" he wondered.

The brief was long, filled with run-on sentences and flowery language about an accused's right to a fair trial and due process and all that jazz. But what it boiled down to was the evidence rule Brunelle was relying on to admit the video, and another provision of that same rule that Khachaturian was going to use to try to suppress it.

Washington Evidence Rule 901(b)(1) said evidence could be authenticated so long as a witness testified 'that a matter is what it is claimed to be.'

Detective Emory, is this a video of the parking garage where Mr. Jenkins was murdered?

Yes, it is.

Boom. Admitted.

But Khachaturian was citing to Section (b)(9) of 901: 'Process or System. Evidence describing a process or system used to produce a result and showing that the process or system produces an accurate result.'

Detective Emory, does the video surveillance in that parking garage use a process or system that accurately records what it purports to record?

Uh. I guess so. I'm not really a tech person.

"Shit," Brunelle exhaled.

Then he picked up the phone and dialed Nicole's extension.

"Yes, David?" she answered.

"What's the name of that video expert we used in that one case a few years back?" he asked.

"Check your email," Nicole answered, her smile almost audible. "I already sent it to you."

Brunelle checked his monitor. Sure enough, there was the email, complete with the expert's name, address, phone, and email.

"I thought I was supposed to tell you what I needed?" Brunelle complained.

Nicole chuckled. "Come on, Dave. You know you're not very good at knowing what you really need."

CHAPTER 8

The office of Maxwell Hutchinson, video expert, was located extremely inconveniently in Portland, Oregon, a good four-hour drive from downtown Seattle. Three-and-a-half, if you sped the whole way. Which Brunelle did, of course. He'd gotten up early, so he arrived in the City of Roses a little after 10:00 a.m.

People from Seattle liked to say Portland is what Seattle was like twenty years earlier. Brunelle imagined Portlanders probably hated hearing that. But, he thought as he looked around, it was true. He was able to find a parking spot on the street just a block from Hutchinson's office. There was a light rain. No one bothered with an umbrella. Food trucks lined the street. It was like a smaller, friendlier version of Seattle. He allowed himself to wonder if the D.A.'s office was hiring.

Hutchinson's office took up half of the top floor of a nondescript office building with a brick façade and an annoying elevator that announced each floor it stopped on.

"Seven," the elevator's soothing female voice told him as he stepped into the hallway and spotted the sign for 'Hutchinson Digital Imagery' to his left. A moment later he was inside the office and the receptionist—a nice young man with a thin beard and slight frame—stood up to fetch his employer.

Brunelle opted not to take a seat. Instead, he decided to peruse the waiting room while he waited. The walls were filled with matted and framed copies of articles featuring Hutchinson. In most of them, he stood with arms crossed, glancing over his shoulder to smile confidently at the camera, looking genius-like with his shortly cropped balding hairline and small round glasses. Brunelle started reading the article closest to him. The byline, supported by the photos of the Brandenburg Gate, was Berlin.

"That was one of my most interesting cases."

Brunelle spun around to see Maxwell Hutchinson, arms uncrossed, but clearly recognizable from the myriad of framed images.

"Oh yeah?" Brunelle encouraged.

"Yes." Hutchinson stepped forward to point at the article under glass. "I was hired by the Berlin Police to review video footage of a young man whom they suspected of perpetrating a series of armed robberies in one of the more dangerous quarters of town. He also happened to be the son of one of the city councilmen and had gone missing several weeks earlier. The conjecture was that he was using the robberies to get enough money to live off of while hiding away in the bad part of town."

Brunelle nodded. Sounded interesting. "So what happened? Was it him?"

"It certainly looked like him when I first reviewed the surveillance videos," Hutchinson answered. "Robbers rarely stop to pose for the camera, but when you viewed the videos from all the different angles, the robber looked remarkably like young Dieter Grossbeck."

"But?" Brunelle asked. There was obviously a 'but.'

"But I wasn't certain," Hutchinson answered. "The images were grainy, the resolution low. I wanted to be sure."

"So what did you do?"

Hutchinson raised a fist to his chin. "I looked elsewhere," he said. "His father was certain he'd fled to that neighborhood, so I asked the police for all the public surveillance video for the area. Streetcar stops, subway stops, traffic cameras, everything. Sure enough I found him. He was living there all right. And I had him on tape entering a U-Bahn station at the exact same time that other fellow was robbing a wurst stand. It didn't take long to track his movements through the neighborhood then, and we found him holed up with an older woman of Turkish ancestry. Apparently, his father didn't approve of the relationship and failed to mention it to me as I set out to figure out what happened, lest it get out that his oh-so-German son was cavorting with a Turk."

"Is that a thing over there?" Brunelle wondered.

"Oh, yes," Hutchinson answered. "Large numbers of Turkish 'guest workers' came to Germany after World War II to help rebuild. They stayed and now their great-grandchildren live there. But they still find themselves both economically and culturally marginalized."

"So socioeconomic factors clouded the investigation and hindered your ability to do your job neutrally and accurately?"

Hutchinson considered the sentence for a moment. "Yes," he agreed.

Brunelle smiled. "Then I've come to the right man."

Hutchinson returned the smile. "And I'm glad you have. I can't wait to tell you what I've been able to do."

Hutchinson led Brunelle back into his offices, which were probably better labeled his 'lab': a large room filled with video screens and computers, with keyboards and mouses and digital pens connected to monitors of all shapes and sizes by an absolute army of crossing and twisting cords. The video Brunelle had forwarded to Hutchinson in advance of their meeting—at Hutchinson's insistence—was queued up on several of the screens, including the largest, which took up most of one of the walls. Brunelle recognized the elevator doors. He knew Rappaport was about to step off. Or at least he hoped it was Rappaport and not some German look-alike.

"Please tell me Rappaport wasn't hanging out in the Turkish district of Bellevue that night," Brunelle quipped.

Hutchinson thought for a moment. "Does Bellevue have a Turkish district?"

Brunelle hesitated. "Uh, I—I don't know. It was kind of a joke."

"Ah," Hutchinson replied. "Well, no. I don't believe I'll need to look at the traffic cameras in Bellevue for that night. I feel comfortable that the man in this video is Neil Rappaport."

Brunelle breathed a sigh of relief. "Well, that's good."

"Yes," Hutchinson replied, "but that's not the best part. The best part is that I was able to confirm the identity using a brand new video resolution enhancing algorithm I developed myself."

Brunelle wasn't sure he liked the sound of that. "You can't tell from just the raw video?" Emory and Tanner had been sure of their identification.

"Yes, well, it's not really an either/or proposition," Hutchinson replied. "I've been waiting for a good test case for my program, and this worked perfectly. Here, let me show you."

Hutchinson stepped over to what appeared to be his control center. Most of the cords made their way, one way or another, to the small monitor and keyboard perched on a table next to several empty coffee cups. "By the way," he said as he started the video with a series of mouse-clicks, "the equipment used to make this video must be some of the best I've ever seen. Almost as good as my own stuff. Usually store surveillance video is middling at best. Most companies don't invest too heavily in the hardware."

"You should see their control room," Brunelle replied. "No expense spared. I thought I was about to see the moon landing or something."

"That wasn't faked, you know," Hutchinson said. "I've reviewed the video myself. It's authentic."

Brunelle wasn't sure how to respond. "Okay."

"Just in case you were curious," Hutchinson added. "Definitely not doctored. Ah, here we are," he announced and paused the video playback just as Rappaport—if that's who it really was—was stepping off the elevator.

A few more mouse-clicks and the image on the large screen zoomed in to isolate Rappaport's face. It was pixilated at that magnification, but not too terrible. Brunelle could see the man's face. He just hadn't known the man well enough to be able to recognize him.

"Pretty good, right?" Hutchinson said. "You can definitely make out some of the facial features."

"Right," Brunelle answered. "And both my detective and the security guy said it was definitely Rappaport."

"Yes, well," Hutchinson answered. "I'm not sure they can say it is definitely him. Not from this unaugmented video, anyway."

Brunelle frowned. He didn't need his expert calling into question the identification of the killer. "Why is that? I thought you said this was top-of-the-line video equipment."

"Oh, it is, it is," Hutchinson assured. "The problem isn't your video equipment, it's your killer. He's too common looking."

Hutchinson pulled up a photo of Rappaport and put it in the upper corner of the screen. It looked to have been downloaded from the internet. Rappaport was smiling and looking at the camera.

"See, he's pretty average-looking," Hutchinson said. "At least demographically speaking. He's a middle-aged white male with dark hair and no noticeable disfigurements." Hutchinson glanced at Brunelle. "Much like you."

Brunelle nodded. "Thanks. It's always nice to hear I don't have any noticeable disfigurements."

Hutchinson nodded. "You're welcome. But when it comes to criminal suspects, disfigurements are the most reliable of identification. Injuries, scars, tattoos, piercings. All of those are highly unique to the individual. If your perpetrator were missing an eye, or had one arm, those would narrow the suspect list considerably."

"Like 'The Fugitive,'" Brunelle offered. "The one-armed man."

"Exactly," Hutchinson replied. "I've often thought that if I were ever going to commit a robbery or similar crime, I would put on a temporary neck or face tattoo. Something that the witnesses would remember and would be used as the way to positively identify the suspect. Then I would simply wash it off. No matter how much I looked like the fellow in the video, everyone would agree it couldn't be me because I don't have a spider-web tattoo covering my neck."

Brunelle nodded. That actually made sense. He'd need to remember that if he ever got a case where the killer was identified by his tattoo.

"But this fellow," Hutchinson gestured to the screen, "he doesn't have anything like that. Is it Neil Rappaport? Well, yes, probably. But the most I could say based on this unenhanced video is that the image is *consistent with* Neil Rappaport."

"I don't like that phrasing," Brunelle commented.

"I wouldn't either, if I were the prosecutor," Hutchinson agreed. "It's weak, equivocal. It definitely leaves room for some doubt, maybe even reasonable doubt."

"You're not making me feel better, Mr. Hutchinson," Brunelle said.

"Please, call me Maxwell," Hutchinson replied. "And that's why it's good you came to me. Watch this."

Brunelle watched the screen as several pop-up windows appeared and Hutchinson adjusted some settings from his place at the control center. After a few moments, he clicked the 'Okay' button on the screen and something amazing happened.

"Voila," Hutchinson announced as the blocky pixels melted and smoothed into a high resolution image of the killer's face. Rappaport's face.

"That's him," Brunelle knew. It was a perfect match. One that made Emory's and Tanner's identification seem like guesswork after all. "How did you do that?"

Hutchinson stepped over to the screen, beaming. "I've been frustrated by the limitations of source video for so long, I can't even tell you. But as I said, most surveillance video is middling at best. So I developed a software program that analyzes each pixel and breaks it down into nine smaller pixels—a three-by-three square— and assigns each sub-pixel a new color or shade based on the colors and shades around the original pixel. It tries several combinations, comparing them to all other combinations of all the other pixels, each one of which is of course connected to all the pixels around it. It's very complicated. And I was only having nominal results with the low-resolution videos I usually work with. But when you sent me this video, I thought the algorithm might actually work. And it did. Perfectly!"

Brunelle looked again at the internet image and the enhanced image of the surveillance video. It was Rappaport. No doubt about it.

"Can you explain to the judge how your system works?" he asked. "And how the original surveillance equipment works? I need you to be able to do that to get it admitted."

Hutchinson let out a light scoff. "Of course I can explain it. The question will be whether the judge can understand it."

"Yeah, don't say that on the stand," Brunelle counseled. But otherwise he was looking forward to calling Hutchinson to the stand to testify against Khachaturian's motion. They wrapped up the session and Hutchinson walked Brunelle to the lobby.

As they shook hands in departure, Hutchinson was grinning broadly, but Brunelle was frowning. Something had occurred to him.

"Is there something wrong?" Hutchinson asked.

"Well, I was just thinking," Brunelle answered. "You said you just developed this software. That means it's brand new. And brand new scientific evidence has to pass something called the *Frye* test."

"I'm familiar with the *Frye* standard," Hutchinson replied. "From the 1923 Supreme Court case *Frye v. United States*. To be admissible in a trial, a novel scientific method must be generally accepted within the relevant scientific community."

"Right," Brunelle nodded. "So," he mused, "how do I establish that, if you're the only one doing this?"

Hutchinson laughed and spread his arms to indicate all of the articles, awards, and trophies decorating his waiting room. "Relax, Mr. Brunelle. I *am* the relevant scientific community."

CHAPTER 9

Brunelle wasn't so sure the self-aggrandizing assertion of one expert was going to be sufficient to overcome Khachaturian's predictable objection to using a new video manipulation method. On the other hand, once it was applied, there was no doubt the murderer was Rappaport. He turned the problem over and over in his mind on the drive back to Seattle. Maybe he could convince Hutchinson to share the software program with other videographers. But he doubted Hutchinson would go along with that. It would undercut his status as the premier expert in the field, and if he could get it to work on the standard, lower-res videos used across the country, and the world, Hutchinson was sitting on a gold mine.

Four hours of rumination didn't lead to any solution and by the time Brunelle fought through the rush hour traffic he'd arrived into and made his way to his condo north of downtown, he was ready for the weekend that had started at five o'clock. He'd been smart to schedule his field trip on a Friday. He just wanted to relax that weekend and do nothing.

But his phone had other plans. Halfway through his glass of

whiskey and the latest installment of his favorite Netflix series, his phone buzzed. A text. From Paul Cross.

Party. My place. Tomorrow night. Starts at 9:00. You're invited. Please come.

Brunelle sighed. Nine o'clock? That seemed awfully late. He was fully feeling his 40-some years.

Sorry. I have to pass, he started typing. A second text arrived before he could finish and hit send.

Vickie will be there

Brunelle stopped typing. Then he backspaced and deleted his original text.

Sounds great. Thanks for the invite. See you tomorrow at 9.

Paul sent a 'thumbs up' emoji in response, and Brunelle stood up from his couch. He drained the rest of his drink and turned off the T.V. If he was going to go to a party that *started* at 9:00 p.m. the next night, he was going to need to go to bed early to stock up on his sleep. He wasn't in college any more.

* * *

Looking back, Brunelle should have guessed there would be a valet. Rich guy, big party, valet parking. It just made sense. Instead he pulled into the driveway to find himself in line to the temporary valet stand set up at the apex of the circle drive in front of Paul Cross's front door. He was in his ten-year-old base model sedan, sandwiched between the latest Tesla SUV in front of him and a Land Rover behind him, and no way back out to the street to self-park. Luckily he'd brought some cash in case Paul had made arrangements for a bar. That much he had anticipated.

When it was his turn he sheepishly exited his vehicle, hoping the fast food wrappers in the back weren't illuminated by the dome light, and handed his keys to the high school kid who stepped up to him in a red vest and black bow tie.

"Good evening, sir," he said in that tenor-like tone young men had before they got used to their lower voices.

Brunelle handed him his keys and pulled a five out of his wallet. "Uh, is this okay?" he asked. "I don't know what the going rate is for this sort of thing."

The young man smiled. "It's a little higher than this," he replied, pleasantly enough. "But no worries. Everybody else is tipping huge. I'm killing it tonight, especially for a high school student."

Brunelle felt both relieved and a little guilty. He distracted himself with a joke. Nodding to the car that had just pulled away and two more of the same model in line behind him. "Do you go to Tesla High?"

"No, sir. I live in Bellevue," the valet replied with a slight frown. "Tesla STEM High School is in Redmond."

Brunelle decided not to try any more jokes. He thanked the young man again, who then pointed to the far edge of Paul Cross's home. "The party is around back. Mr. Cross emptied out his garage for the valet parking and parked his own cars along the drive there. You can follow them to the pool area where the hostess will greet you."

Brunelle frowned slightly himself. "Thanks," he said. And then he made his way toward the side of the house, amid the other partygoers who were arriving, but walking decidedly slower than any of them. Word of a pool complex only confirmed he was a fish out of water.

To make way for the other guests who were hurrying to join the festivities, Brunelle stepped closer to the line of vehicles Paul had collected and inspected them as he passed. He had his own Tesla of course—two in fact, an older sedan and a new SUV. Both white. There was a silver BMW convertible, a black Audi sedan, and a lime green sports car that looked more Hollywood prop than actual motor vehicle. When he reached that one, he only had to look at the hood to see the manufacturer's name emblazoned on it.

"Lotus," he murmured to himself, with a small shake of the head. *Wasn't that another name for marijuana?* he thought he remembered.

After the Lotus were a few more sports cars and convertibles, and then Brunelle finally reached the hostess stand. It was set up in front of the gate to the 'pool complex,' which, it turned out, was accurately named. There wasn't just one pool; there were three. With at least as many outbuildings. From the lights inside, one of them seemed to house a fourth, indoor pool. The others were smaller, huts of some sort, their uses undeterminable from that distance.

"Hello. Welcome to the party," the hostess greeted him as he reached the gate. She was a young woman—older than the high school students out front, to be sure—but likely just over the legal drinking age. Even if only because Brunelle could see the bar behind her and supposed whatever company Paul had hired to cater the event knew about the regulations regarding minors working in areas where liquor was sold. Ah, the things one knew from practicing criminal law. "Can I get your name, please?"

"Dave Brunelle," he answered, pausing his gait to allow her to check the guest list on her podium. It only took a moment.

"Ah, yes," she said with a smile. "There you are." She gestured beyond her. "Enjoy the party."

Brunelle assured her he would as he entered, even if he wasn't so sure himself. He wasn't much of a party guy. And he definitely wasn't a rich party guy. Paul's home had seemed modest the night of the murder. It turned out, he just hadn't seen the whole place. So a 'pool complex' full of rich, Tesla-driving Eastsiders wasn't really his thing. Especially when he didn't know any of them.

He went over to the bar.

"Hey there," he greeted the bartender, a man probably about his same age, with graying hair slicked straight back from his face. He wore a white coat and the same black bow tie the valet had sported. "Can I just get a bourbon? Neat."

"Sure thing." The bartender pointed to the wall of bottles set up behind him. "Do you have a favorite brand?"

Brunelle shook his head. "No. Just something with alcohol. Surprise me."

Soon enough the bartender slid a glass with an inch or so of brown liquid courage over to Brunelle and Brunelle reached for his wallet.

But the bartender waved him off. "It's an open bar, sir. Mr. Cross is paying." Then he added, as if realizing how out of place Brunelle was and wanting to make sure he knew even the hired help was more in tune with things than he was, "Of course."

Brunelle grimaced as he pushed his wallet back into his pocket. "Of course," he parroted. Then he turned and scanned the scene. Maybe there was somebody he recognized after all. Somebody else from college. Somebody else he'd dated in a whirlwind romance. Somebody who looked like they were feeling as awkward as he was.

But no such luck. He didn't recognize anyone. And they all seemed to be enjoying themselves. Groups of threes and fours and fives held lively conversations at various spots between the pools, which were lit up from within. Brunelle supposed Paul must be somewhere in the crowd. He hoped Vickie was too. He took a deep drink of his bourbon and headed into the fray.

Brunelle might not have liked parties full of people he didn't know, but he was still a trial attorney, and trial attorneys were showmen. He turned on that charm he usually reserved for jurors and walked up to the first group he encountered.

"Dave."

"A friend of Paul's."

"We went to college together."

"I'm a lawyer."

"No, not patents. I'm a prosecutor."

And the group quickly broke apart.

Brunelle frowned inside, but decided to keep walking. Another group, another set of introductions.

"Dave Brunelle."

"Paul and I were roommates in college."

"Lawyer."

"No, I don't work for Paul."

"Actually, I'm a prosecutor with King County."

And that group also dissolved.

Mercifully, as Brunelle was approaching his third group, and already finishing that first drink, Paul came hurrying over to greet him.

"Dave!" He almost shouted as he navigated the corner of one of the pools, his own drink extended upward lest anything spill. "You made it. I'm so glad."

Brunelle reached out and shook Paul's hand. "Thanks for inviting me." Then with a self-deprecating smile, "And rescuing me. I don't seem to be making many friends."

Paul put his arm around Brunelle's shoulder and started guiding him back toward the main house. "Nonsense," he assured. "It's just that most of these folks already know each other. We have a lot of these parties, and it's mostly the same people on the guest list each time."

Brunelle nodded. That made sense.

"Also," Paul continued, "you might not want to tell them you're a prosecutor. I kinda forgot to tell you that."

Brunelle stopped walking. "What? Why?"

Then he could guess why. He turned around at the other partygoers. "Oh shit, Paul. Are there drugs here?"

Paul shrugged. "It's a party, Dave."

Brunelle looked around again, his eyes widening a bit. "Shit, Paul. I can't be here if there are drugs around. What if the cops bust the party? I can't get caught at a party with drugs. I could lose my job."

But Paul laughed. "The cops," he assured Brunelle, "aren't busting this party, Dave. The cops don't bust my parties, or any of the parties of the other people here. Besides, most of the drugs here are pills and somebody probably has a prescription for some of them somewhere."

"Great, I'm at a party with a bunch of pill-poppers." Brunelle ran a hand over his head.

"Hey, hey, watch it there, pal," Paul shot back. 'These are my friends you're talking about. They work hard, really hard, making the products that run this fucking country. They deserve to blow off some steam after a long week."

Brunelle set his empty glass down on a nearby table. "Fine. We can talk about the legalization of drugs some other time. But until then, I better go. I haven't actually seen anything yet. If I do, I would probably have to report it so I don't lose my job."

Paul reached out and patted him on the shoulder. "Relax, Dave. Really. You aren't going to see anything. It's not some drug orgy with people pouring pills down their throats. Just don't walk in on anyone in the bathroom. Which, come to think of it, is pretty good advice no matter what."

Brunelle relaxed, even if just slightly. "Yeah," he acknowledged Paul's joke. "But still, I probably better leave."

Paul frowned. "But I wanted to hear how the case against Neil was going?"

Brunelle frowned slightly himself. The other partygoers might have been blowing off steam, but apparently he was still working.

"And Vic wanted to see you," Paul added. "I can't let you go without at least saying hi to her. She let me have it when you just left that morning without saying goodbye. You told her you wouldn't and then you did, and you're damn well not doing it again."

Brunelle sighed. But he remembered why he'd really come to the party. "The case is going fine," he assured Paul. "It's early still. Not much has happened yet. It will get more intense as we approach the trial date."

"Okay, well, keep me in the loop," Paul requested. "I have lawyers on standby to file papers as soon as Neil is convicted. When we set up the business, we put a clause in the partnership agreement that if either of us died or became permanently disabled, that partner's half would automatically transfer to the other. I'm going to argue that life in prison is permanently disabled."

Brunelle shook his head. "It won't be life. The standard range is twenty to twenty-five years, plus five for the gun. Thirty years tops."

"Same difference," Paul replied. "We're not in college any more, Dave. Neil won't live thirty more years, especially not in prison. At least that's what we're going to argue."

"Great." Brunelle wasn't really interested in partnership law. He'd opted for a trial advocacy clinic over the standard business law class during law school. He looked past Paul toward the house.

"So where's Vickie?"

Paul smiled. He didn't seem all that interested in the case after all. No follow-up questions at all. Instead, he said, "Stay here. I'll go get her."

"Maybe I'll head inside too," Brunelle countered. "In case people start pouring pills down their throats."

Paul shook his head. "Fine. Suit yourself." He pointed at the open bar. "But do us both a favor and get another drink."

Brunelle decided he couldn't argue with that.

A few minutes later found Brunelle sitting on a leather couch in a type of room he didn't even know the name for, his second drink half-drunk, and himself not too far off from that either. Then Paul and Vickie walked into the room.

At least it was probably Paul. He wasn't really visible to Brunelle in the glare surrounding Vickie. Seeing her in her pajamas at three in the morning had been exhilarating enough, but viewing her dressed for a party—Brunelle could hardly breathe. Her hair was pulled back and up, showing off the strong lines of her face and neck. Her black dress hugged her curvy frame, and her long legs strode confidently toward him as he tried to regain his voice.

"Dave Brunelle," she said with a playful scowl. "You owe me an apology."

"Oh-okay," Brunelle managed to reply as he stood up. "Whatever you say."

Vickie laughed. "You haven't changed in twenty years, Dave. For good and bad."

Brunelle nodded. She really did look great. Why hadn't they stayed together?

"You said you wouldn't leave without saying goodbye," she reminded him. "But when I came back down not ten minutes later, you were gone. And no goodbye."

The specificity of the memory brought Brunelle back to his senses. "Uh, right. Yeah, sorry about that. I was kind of in the middle of a case. I had to go."

"Go and arrest my ex-husband," Vickie expounded.

"Uh, yeah," Brunelle agreed. "Small world."

Vickie laughed at that. Before she or Brunelle could say anything, Paul—it really was him—jumped in.

"I better get back out to my guests," he said.

Brunelle ignored him. Vickie did too. So he nodded to himself and took his leave.

"Wait." Brunelle realized something. "Was I supposed to apologize for leaving without saying goodbye? Or for arresting your ex-husband? Because, technically, the detective did that."

Another light laugh. "You don't need to apologize for arresting Neil. He can go to jail, or Hell, or wherever, for all I care. The split had been a long time coming. We had problems like anybody else, and then some. But the way he did it. Just all of a sudden, out of nowhere, and with that ultimatum: don't fight it and you'll get everything you want." She shook her head. "I don't know what happened to him all of a sudden. But I've decided I'm not going to care either. And if he killed somebody, then he belongs in prison."

"So, definitely the no goodbye thing," Brunelle confirmed.

"Definitely the no goodbye thing," Vickie answered. "So don't go pulling that crap again tonight."

Brunelle nodded. "Okay. Well, then I better say goodbye now. I was just getting ready to leave."

Vickie's face fell. "What? Why?"

Brunelle pointed toward the 'pool complex.' "Apparently, it's a pill orgy out there. I can't really be here if there are crimes being committed. Kind of conflicts with the whole prosecutor gig."

"Oh yeah," Vickie answered. She didn't seem surprised by the drugs, just his inability to be around it. "Well, did you actually see anyone using?"

"No." Brunelle shook his head. "Not yet. But I don't want to wait for it to happen. Besides," he half smiled, "I don't think I was very popular once I told people what I did for a living. The party will probably go better without me."

"Maybe for the others," Vickie answered. "But not for me." She reached out and took his hand. "Come on. Let's go someplace where you can look at something besides Paul's friends popping pills."

She pulled him toward the staircase leading upstairs. He let himself be pulled, wondering exactly what he was going to get to look at, and knowing what he was hoping for.

In the event, it turned out not to be anything under that tight black dress he followed up the stairs. Instead, it was a breathtaking view of Lake Washington and the Seattle skyline beyond, from an upstairs balcony off what Brunelle figured was best described as a study. Or maybe a library. There were books, and leather chairs. And a balcony with a view of Seattle.

"Isn't it magnificent?" Vickie asked as she leaned onto the railing.

Brunelle looked at her lithe and relaxed form draped on the balcony, then turned to look at the buildings lit up across the water. "It sure is." He stepped forward and joined her in leaning on the rail. "Do you come up here a lot?"

"I have since I moved in with Paul," Vickie answered. "We had a similar view at my house with Neil. I used to go up there all the time. To get away from the kids. To get away from Neil. To just be by myself for a few minutes and try to remember who I am. You can really lose yourself in a marriage."

Brunelle wasn't sure what to say. He offered an unknowing shrug. "Yeah, I would guess so."

Vickie stood up. "Oh, I'm sorry. I didn't mean to start talking about Neil, or my kids. Let's talk about you for a minute. Is there a Mrs. Brunelle?"

"My mom," Brunelle quipped. "But no. No Mrs. Brunelle. No Davey Juniors either. It's just me." He glanced out again at the view. "I can look at the skyline any time I want."

"Do you?" Vickie asked.

Brunelle considered for a moment. "No. Not really. I don't have anyone I need to get away from. Besides, I don't have this view. The balcony of my condo looks out at more condos."

"Oh, yeah," Vickie replied. "I hadn't thought about that. But I guess that wasn't what I was really asking. So, no Mrs. Brunelle. But there must have been something serious, right?"

Brunelle shrugged and looked at her. "They're all serious at the time, right?"

She demurred. "Not all of them."

Brunelle laughed. "Yeah, okay, not all of them. But most of them. The ones you want to see a second time. It's all very serious. Probably too serious." He looked out at the water again. "Maybe that's what makes it not work. I don't know."

"None of us do, Dave," Vickie answered. "You don't get much more serious than married with two kids. But here I am." She paused. "And here you are."

He turned back to her. If she'd changed any since college, he didn't see it. It didn't matter. Seriously.

So, of course, he said, "I should go."

Vickie sighed. "Really? Again? Now?"

"Yeah," Brunelle looked away. "I probably shouldn't even

be here."

"Because of the drugs?"

"No," Brunelle said. "Because of the case. I'm not sure I should be standing on a balcony looking at the stars with the defendant's wife."

"Ex-wife," Vickie reminded him. "And we're looking at the city, not the stars. It's overcast tonight."

"You always were smarter than me," Brunelle deflected.

"That's true," Vickie answered. Then she reached out and touched his arm. "Go ahead and say good night, then, Dave. But don't say goodbye just yet. We have a lot of time to catch up on. Sometime."

Brunelle thought for a moment. "Okay, sometime," he agreed. "I'd like that." He stood up straight again. "Good night, Vickie."

She stood up, too, and kissed him lightly on the cheek. "Good night, Dave."

CHAPTER 10

The good part about seeing Vickie again was, well, seeing Vickie again. The bad part was that Brunelle couldn't keep her out of his head, even as he should have been preparing for Khachaturian's motion to suppress the video. Luckily, Nicole had stepped in to help, so Hutchinson had gotten his subpoena and knew when and where to show up for the hearing. But even on the morning of the hearing, Brunelle's head wasn't completely in the game.

"Mr. Brunelle," Hutchinson immediately greeted him from the back of the gallery as he walked into the courtroom. "Nice to see you again."

Brunelle feigned focus. "Mr. Hutchinson. Good to see you too. Thanks for coming."

Hutchinson wasn't the only person sitting in the gallery. Brunelle was a bit surprised, but pleased, to see that Det. Emory had come to watch the hearing. He was less excited to see Beverly and Tom Jenkins. He didn't need the extra dimension of an audience. Or rather a second audience. Public speaking was all about knowing your audience, but a judge was different from the victim's family. A judge wanted detached, fair advocacy. The victim's family wanted blood and screaming. Trying to balance both audiences made it difficult to address either one well.

But Brunelle knew not to let his consternation show on his face. And he knew to contact them first, before Emory.

"Beverly," he extended a hand to the victim's mother, before offering it next to his brother. "Tom. Thanks for coming today."

"I told you we're gonna come to every hearing," Beverly answered from her scooter parked at the end of the first row of seats.

Brunelle didn't recall her actually saying that, but he demurred. "And I'm glad. It's always good for the judge to see the victim hasn't been forgotten."

Tom skipped the pleasantries. He narrowed his eyes at the defense table. Rappaport sat calmly enough in what Brunelle guessed was an outrageously expensive suit, and was surrounded by all three of his attorneys. "How come he's got three lawyers and we only got one?"

"We only need one," Brunelle replied confidently, although he regretted the boast almost immediately. *Underpromise and overdeliver*, he reminded himself. "Or maybe he just thinks he'll need that many to have any chance. Either way, it doesn't matter. The evidence is the evidence. We have him on videotape."

Tom nodded at that. "What's today's hearing for anyway? We saw it on the court's website, but it just said 'motion.' What's the motion?"

Brunelle half-smiled. "To suppress the videotape."

As Tom and Beverly took a moment to process that answer, Brunelle took the opportunity to extricate himself. "I better get ready. The judge will be out any minute."

He turned toward the prosecution table and nodded at

Emory to join him there. She said hello to the Jenkinses as she passed and stepped up to Brunelle as he set up his file and rulebooks on the table.

"Thanks for coming," Brunelle said. "I didn't expect to see you here. The family, maybe, but I'm not usually honored with the presence of my lead detective until the actual trial."

"Are you kidding?" Emory replied. "I wanted to see you in action."

Brunelle smiled.

"I mean," she continued, "if you suck, I'd like to know that before the trial."

"Great." The smile faded. "Glad you came. Really."

Emory laughed. "C'mon, Dave. I'm just kidding. I can read you, remember? You're nervous. Relax. I trust you completely. You got this."

Brunelle returned the smile. "Thanks." Then he added, "I better have this. All I have to do today is prove a videotape is an accurate depiction of what the camera recorded."

"Whoa," Emory half-laughed. "Did you say 'video*tape*'?"

Brunelle's eyebrows knitted together. "Uh, yeah?"

"How old are you?' Emory asked. "It hasn't been tape for a couple of decades now."

Brunelle sighed. "Fine. Videodisk, or whatever. Gosh, did I mention I'm really glad you came?"

But Emory just smiled. "You will be when you don't call it videotape in front of the family and the judge. You're welcome."

Before Brunelle could figure out how, or whether, to reply, the judge took the bench and the attorneys snapped to attention.

"All rise!" the bailiff commanded. "The King County Superior Court is now in session, The Honorable Catherine Nguyen presiding."

Judge Nguyen strode into the courtroom and took her seat above the litigants. "Are the parties ready to proceed in the matter of The State of Washington versus Neil Rappaport?"

Brunelle stood up first. "The State is ready, Your Honor."

Nguyen had made a career out of being a jurist. Brunelle had heard she'd done a year or two of private practice after law school, but then she got a job as a District Court Commissioner, spending day after day hearing speeding tickets and contested tows. She'd worked her way up from there, first to full blown District Court Judge, then to Superior Court Judge. Rumor had it, she was a favorite to get the next appointment to the Court of Appeals. So, while she didn't have the experience of a recently appointed or elected litigator, she had vast experience doing the job she was doing right then. She knew the evidence rules as well as anyone.

And there was no way she was going to suppress a videotape of a murder. Not on Khachaturian's current claims, anyway.

The defense attorney stood up next. They always answered second. "The defense is ready, Your Honor," Khachaturian confirmed.

Judge Nguyen nodded. "All right then. This is a defense motion, but the State is the proponent of the proffered evidence. So, Mr. Brunelle, I believe the burden is on you. You go first."

Brunelle was still standing. You always stood to address a judicial officer, District Court Commissioner or Superior Court Judge. "By way of a brief opening statement, the State intends to show that the process used to record the defendant committing the murder in this case—"

"Objection!" It was Voegel who stood up to interrupt Brunelle. "There is no evidence that my client was the one who murdered the alleged victim that night."

Judge Nguyen frowned at the objection. But she turned to Brunelle for an answer.

"Uh," Brunelle started. He wasn't used to being objected to in his opening statement, let alone at a preliminary hearing where the evidence rules didn't even apply. And even less so for the reason given. "Well, Your Honor, I think that's why we're here. To discuss which evidence will be admissible to show that Mr. Rappaport is the one who murdered Gerald Jenkins. And he's not an alleged victim. He was shot in the back of the head. He's a victim. The only question is whether Mr. Rappaport pulled the trigger, and the State submits that the videotape shows just that."

Nguyen thought for a moment, then looked again at Voegel. But she didn't address the objection. Not yet anyway. "Mr. Voegel," she asked, "are you going to be presenting an opening statement or a closing argument, or doing the examination of any of the witnesses today?"

Voegel, who had stood to object, shifted his weight slightly. "Uh, no, Your Honor. Mr. Khachaturian will be conducting the hearing today."

The judge nodded. "Then any objections should be coming from him." She looked to the criminal defense attorney. "Do you have an objection, Mr. Khachaturian?"

Khachaturian stood up. "No, Your Honor." He didn't look at Voegel, or Walker for that matter.

So, possibly some dissention in the ranks, Brunelle deduced. Or hoped, anyway.

Judge Nguyen nodded again. "Thank you, Mr. Khachaturian. You may proceed, Mr. Brunelle."

Brunelle thought for a moment. "I think that's all I really had to say, Your Honor. The videotape is accurate." Then, "Video-disk.

Video-recording." He took a breath. "May I just go ahead and call my witness?"

Nguyen allowed a small smile. "Go ahead, Mr. Brunelle."

Brunelle turned around and gestured at Hutchinson to come forward, even as he announced, "The State calls Maxwell Hutchinson to the stand."

Hutchinson stood up and came forward to be sworn in by the judge. In short order, he was seated on the witness stand and Brunelle started his direct-examination.

"Could you state your name for the record?"

The problem with direct-exam, especially at a pretrial hearing with no jury present, and even more so on an issue that he knew he was all but guaranteed to win, was that it wasn't particularly interesting. Even with the victim family in the room. So, even as Hutchinson told the judge his name, Brunelle's mind started to wander.

"And how are you employed, sir?"

It didn't help that Brunelle already knew the answers to these initial introductory questions.

"And what exactly is a Digital and Analog Video-Recording Consultant?"

The judge needed to hear it, and it needed to be in the record, but the bottom line was Hutchinson knew how video-recording worked.

"Have you ever testified as an expert before regarding video-recording technology?"

Of course he had. That's why Brunelle had called him.

Up to that point, Brunelle had trouble paying attention because he knew the answers already. Next, he would have trouble because he *didn't* know the answers. Or understand them.

"Could you explain to the Court how video-recording

technology works, generally speaking?"

Brunelle was a lawyer, not a scientist, or a techie. He knew how to point and shoot a camera, but that was it. That was why he went to law school and didn't become an engineer, or a software developer like Rappaport and Paul Cross. If he had, maybe he could have had a house on the water with three pools and a gaggle of pill-popping friends. And Vickie.

Hutchinson had stopped talking.

"Did you examine the video-recording equipment used by Lincoln Properties regarding this criminal investigation?"

Vickie. She always looked best surrounded by luxury. No, not best. Most comfortable. Most at home. Like she was a part of the luxury, rather than its occupant.

"Do you have an opinion as to whether that particular equipment utilized a process or system which was capable of producing an accurate video recording of the events in that parking garage that night?"

"Yes," Hutchinson answered.

Maybe that's why it didn't work out. Brunelle wasn't luxurious. He was average. He could visit the lakefront villa, but ultimately, he had to leave.

"And what is your opinion?"

Hutchinson looked up at the judge. "The video-recording system used by Lincoln Properties on the date in question was capable of accurately recording, and in fact did accurately record, the events depicted in the recording for that night."

Brunelle nodded at the completion of his examination. "Thank you. No further questions."

It wasn't his most inspired lawyering, but it wasn't the most inspiring issue. Khachaturian could force him to respond to his motions, but he couldn't make him care.

The defense attorney stood up for his cross-examination. He took a few steps toward Hutchinson, waited a second too long, then began.

"The entire purpose of surveillance video," he asked, "is to be able to identify perpetrators after the fact, isn't that correct?"

Hutchinson thought for a moment. "That's one purpose," he agreed. "Although there may be others."

Khachaturian ignored the other reasons. "So, if that's the purpose of surveillance video," he said, "but a particular video recording is too grainy or distant or low resolution to be able to identify a suspect, then the recording system has failed its primary purpose, correct?"

"Uh," Hutchinson replied, "I'm not sure about that. The equipment captures images—"

"And here," Khachaturian interrupted, "the quality of the video is too poor to positively identify the suspect, isn't that true?"

"Well," Hutchinson looked up to the judge again, "*I* can identify him."

Oh, shit, Brunelle thought. *Here we go*. He was paying attention now.

Khachaturian paused. Up until then, he had done a good job of controlling the witness. Good cross-examination consisted not of asking questions, but rather making statements and getting the witness to agree with them. Not, 'What color is the sky?' but 'The sky is blue, right?'

But when the witness volunteers something unexpected? That was different.

"What do you mean?" Khachaturian invited, his face eager for the additional information about to spill out of Hutchinson's even more eager face.

"Well, as I mentioned earlier, I am perhaps the world's

leading authority on digital recording technology." Hutchinson looked around to not just the judge, but anyone lucky enough to be near him at that exact moment. Brunelle, lowered his head into his hand and pretended to take notes. "One of the inherent limits on digital recording is what is known as resolution, that is, the number of pixels in an image. The lower the resolution, the less pixels. That's what causes images to look like collections of squares piled on top of each other. Well, I recently developed a computer software algorithm which…"

Hutchinson then explained his software, in pretty much the same terms he had used to explain it to Brunelle back in Portland. The bottom line was he could enhance the video, and he could identify the shooter.

"…so using the algorithm, I am able to identify Mr. Rappaport as the person in the recording."

There was a pause before Khachaturian continued. Brunelle looked up, expecting any number of reactions. A motion to exclude for violating the *Frye* standard for scientific reliability. A motion for sanctions for failing to disclose this additional information prior to the hearing, followed perhaps by a motion to dismiss for governmental conduct. Something. But instead, he got nothing.

Khachaturian nodded to the judge. "No further questions, Your Honor."

Nguyen appeared just as surprised as Brunelle. She'd also girded for some sort of theatrical outburst from the defense attorney. It was obvious from the questioning, Khachaturian had been caught off guard. Now, she and Brunelle were the ones off guard. After a moment, she looked down at Brunelle and asked the standard question at that point in any witness's testimony. "Any redirect-examination?"

Hell, no, Brunelle knew. That would allow recross-examination. He could end Hutchinson's testimony by standing up and saying, "No, Your Honor. The witness can be excused."

"Any further witnesses?" the judge followed up.

"No, Your Honor," Brunelle answered.

"Any witnesses from the defense?" she asked Khachaturian.

He echoed Brunelle. "No, Your Honor."

Nguyen nodded to herself. "Okay. Argument? Mr. Brunelle?"

Brunelle stood up. It was a simple issue. He wouldn't win or lose based on his argument. Hutchinson had said the magic words: the video system accurately recorded the events of that night. And there were no witnesses who said anything to the contrary. "The State believes we have satisfied the requirements of Evidence Rule 901 and would ask the Court to deny the defense motion to suppress. Thank you."

Khachaturian was next. "We would waive argument, Your Honor, and rely on the wisdom of this good Court. Thank you."

Judge Nguyen waited for the attorneys to both be seated again, then she delivered the ruling that everyone expected. "The defense has filed a motion to suppress the video recording in this case, alleging that the State will be unable to satisfy the requirement of authentication under Evidence Rule 901(b)(10) regarding systems and processes. The State responded with the testimony of a video recording expert, Mr. Hutchinson. Mr. Hutchinson testified, *among other things*," she made sure they knew she'd heard it too, "that he inspected the equipment in this case, as well as the recording, and in his opinion, the system used did produce an accurate result. Accordingly, I will deny the defense motion to suppress the video recording." Then she added, "At least on this ground."

A shot across Brunelle's bow. He knew not to acknowledge it. "Thank you, Your Honor."

The judge departed again to her chambers, and the litigants and spectators were left to find their way out of the courtroom.

Emory came up to Brunelle as he was packing up his things. "Good job," she said. "I knew you'd do it."

Brunelle smiled. He wasn't in the mood to reply with a witty remark. Instead, he just said, "Thanks."

She slapped him on the shoulder and took her leave. He went next to Beverly and Tom Jenkins in the gallery, hoping they hadn't noticed what was an elephant-in-the-room to him, Khachaturian, and Judge Nguyen.

"We won, right?" Beverly asked from her scooter.

"Yes, we won," Brunelle confirmed. "I thought we would, but you still have to do the hearing."

"So the video is in?" Tom asked. "The jury is gonna see it and that expert guy is gonna tell them it was Rappaport, right?"

"The video may or may not come in," Brunelle cautioned. "We won this hearing, but that doesn't mean there won't be others. The video is our best piece of evidence, so they're going to do everything they can to knock it out. But we won today, and that's what matters."

He didn't address whether Hutchinson would be able to identify Rappaport.

"But shouldn't they have to bring all their attacks at once?" Tom pressed. "That doesn't seem fair to keep attacking it. They should attack, and you should win, and that should be the end of it."

Brunelle sympathized. "I can't disagree. But that's not how it works. Everything with lawyers is more complicated than it needs to be, and even more so in criminal cases. He has the right to defend himself, and I have the duty to convict him anyway. I will do my best to do that. Today was important, but we're not done yet."

It was a nice little speech. Luckily, he didn't have to deliver another. "Leave the man alone," Beverly scolded. "He's on our side, and he did a great job. He won today and he'll win again later too. He'll get justice for Jerry."

Brunelle grimaced slightly. It was hard to underpromise when the victim's family made their own promises to themselves. It was a natural part of mourning—but it didn't make it any easier for Brunelle to win the case.

"Thank you, Ms. Jenkins," he said. "We'll let you know when the next hearing is. But I better go thank Mr. Hutchinson for testifying now."

They excused Brunelle with a few more "Thank you"s and an "Of course," and Brunelle made his way to the back of the courtroom where Hutchinson was waiting for him.

"I thought I'd get to talk more about my algorithm," Hutchinson started, not trying to hide his disappointment. "It really is quite remarkable."

"Yeah, well, that wasn't really what today's hearing was about," Brunelle responded. "It was just about their system working, not what you could do to make it even better."

"I suppose," Hutchinson allowed.

Before he could say any more, Brunelle said, "I'm going to need everything you have about your algorithm. It's part of the case now and I have an obligation under the court rules to hand it over to the defense."

"Well, I'm not sure I can give you *everything*," Hutchinson replied. "Some of it is proprietary. I haven't finished securing the patent yet. That takes a rather long time, I'm afraid."

"I misspoke," Brunelle responded. "I have an obligation under the Constitution to turn that information over to the defense. You need to give it to me."

Hutchinson took in a breath to argue, but then seemed to remember who his main clients were. Not good for business to alienate law enforcement. "I'm sure I can make something work. Give me a few days to review everything and I will send you the information."

Brunelle nodded. "Thanks. I don't mean to be harsh, but I don't have any wiggle room on that. And I don't want a murderer to walk because of some avoidable discovery violation."

Hutchinson confirmed his understanding and the two parted on slightly less friendly terms than they'd started the day on. Brunelle would work to patch that up before the trial, but he had one more person he needed to talk to before they left the courtroom.

"Mr. Khachaturian," he said, walking up to the defense table where Khachaturian was just finishing packing up his things. Voegel and Walker had already left with their client. Everyone was gone except for the two lawyers.

"Sorry about that," Brunelle started. "I knew about his software algorithm or whatever, but I didn't think it would come up in this hearing. Honestly, I don't know if it will pass *Frye*, so I hadn't decided whether I was going to pursue it. That's why I didn't get you the information before. But I'll get it now and provide it to you as soon as possible."

Khachaturian snapped his briefcase shut. "I know you will."

Brunelle decided to see if he could connect a little. He usually got along fine with the defense bar. Too well, sometimes.

"So why this motion?" he asked. "You had to know I'd meet ER 901. It's a really low standard."

"Of course I knew," Khachaturian admitted. "But it forced you to put on part of your case in advance. There's no downside for me. If, by some miracle, I win, then the video is suppressed. If, as expected, I lose, well, I still got to preview your evidence. Or, in this case, expose it. Either way, regardless of the ruling, it's a win for me."

Brunelle could understand the logic, even if he didn't like it. "Well, like I said, I'll get that report over to you right away. No need to note a motion over that."

"Oh, Mr. Brunelle," Khachaturian shook his head at him. "Don't ever tell me what motions to file."

CHAPTER 11

"You don't get to tell me what motions to file," Brunelle was still murmuring to himself in a smarmy sing-song days after the hearing. "Some people," he thought aloud. "You try to be nice…"

He knew another motion was coming. And he knew what it was going to be. He could even guess when it would get filed. He'd gotten at least the preliminary materials from Hutchinson two days after the hearing. Nicole had scanned and emailed them to Khachaturian, following up with a same-day courier delivery of a CD with the same materials. Assuming Khachaturian used the weekend to review everything, then needed a few days to find his own expert to review Hutchinson's work, and that expert was good enough to have other clients and therefore be busy with other projects, Brunelle figured it would be about two weeks before he saw the defense motion to prevent Hutchinson from using his refinement algorithm to identify Rappaport as the shooter.

He was wrong on every count.

The motion was waiting for him three days later, neatly centered in front of his chair when he arrived at work that morning. Nicole's handiwork.

The motion did not seek to suppress testimony about Hutchinson's algorithm. It didn't even mention it.

And it moved to exclude Hutchinson's testimony altogether, as unhelpful to the jury—a requirement for expert testimony to be relevant, and therefore admissible.

"What does it say?" Nicole was suddenly standing in his doorway.

Brunelle was still standing in front of his chair, holding the motion in that sweet spot, just far enough to be able to read it without squinting. "It's a motion to exclude Hutchinson's testimony."

Nicole rolled her eyes. "I can read the caption, Dave." The pleading was titled, 'Motion to Exclude Testimony of State's Expert (Hutchinson).' "But why? What's the basis?"

Brunelle raised an eyebrow. "You couldn't read that part?"

Nicole smiled. "I didn't get a chance. It just came in on the fax. I made a copy for myself and put the original on your desk. But you came in early today, and so I haven't had a chance to read the argument yet. What are they claiming? Hutchinson isn't qualified or something?"

Brunelle shook his head. "No, he concedes that Hutchinson is one of the preeminent experts on video recording technology."

"So why shouldn't he be allowed to testify?"

Brunelle shrugged. "Basically, they're arguing that you don't need an expert to decide who's in the video. The jury can just look and make their own decision."

Nicole opened her mouth to argue, but paused. "That's actually kind of a good point," she admitted.

Brunelle's mouth twisted into a frown. "Yeah, but I don't think it should mean Hutchinson can't give his opinion too. He's a lot more practiced at identifying people from videotape."

"Videotape?" Nicole half-laughed. "What is it, 1993? Do you have VHS or Betamax?"

Brunelle sighed. "Video recording," he corrected himself. "And either way, Hutchinson has practice doing that. He could talk about that German thing he did."

Nicole smiled. "That almost sounds dirty."

Brunelle shook his head. "Sorry, Nicole. I'm in no mood. This case is bugging me. I shouldn't have to spend time responding to bullshit motions just because the defense attorney files them."

"But you do?" Nicole confirmed.

"Yes, I do," Brunelle admitted. "Which sucks."

He looked again at the brief in his hand. "And listen to this: 'Additionally, Mr. Hutchinson should not be allowed to provide his allegedly expert opinion as to the identity of the suspect on the video. The identity of the victim's killer is the central question in this case. Therefore, providing an opinion as to that identity would invade the province of the jury.'"

He scoffed and looked up at Nicole, who didn't seem to fully appreciate his disdain.

"'Invade the province of the jury,'" he repeated. "That hasn't been the standard since before I was licensed. Witnesses are allowed to invade the province of the jury. That's all they do. They tell the jury what they think the jury should do. I remember when I started, all the old prosecutors would say," he made a silly expression and took on a tone to match, "'invades the province of the jury,' but now—"

"Now you're the old prosecutor," Nicole interrupted, with a grin.

Brunelle just stared at her for a moment. "Well, thank you."

"Oh, don't pout," Nicole told him. "I was only kidding. Sort of. At least you're getting closer to that sweet government pension of yours."

"Great. Thanks for the reminder," Brunelle answered. "I can't wait to sit at home, eating dinner at 4:30 off of a T.V. tray."

Nicole's grin returned. "What's a T.V. tray?"

"And you can leave now, Ms. Richards," Brunelle said formally. "Your services will no longer be needed this morning."

Nicole laughed, but followed the instruction to depart. "Let me know when you need me to copy, file, and serve the response you'll spend the entire day writing," she called out from down the hall.

"Yes, Ms. Richards," Brunelle called back. "Thank you, Ms. Richards. That'll be all, Ms. Richards."

He finally plopped down into his desk chair, Khachaturian's motion still in his hand.

"What a waste of time," he said as he flipped it on his desk. "I'm wasting time."

He thought for a moment, that mind of his wandering again. "I'm wasting time," he repeated.

Then he pulled out his phone and typed a text. To Vickie Not-Rappaport Cross.

Sometime = Friday? Dinner? You pick the place

CHAPTER 12

Brunelle felt some trepidation at having invited Vickie to choose the restaurant for their rendezvous. He feared they'd end up at some high-end steakhouse, atop one of Bellevue's downtown office towers, with a 360-degree view of water and mountains. Instead, though, they ended up at 'The Crab Shack,' housed in its own, rambling one-story building, with a buckling asphalt parking lot and what was probably once a nice view of Lake Washington— before the luxury condos blocking that view were built.

He parked his car in the remnants of a puddle trapped by the asphalt, and climbed the creaking stairs to the lobby. He'd never been there before—he'd never even heard of it—but from the looks of it inside, it was running a brisk business. It was old-school Seattle—or Bellevue—harkening back to the days, pre-tech-boom, when most of the people there made their living one way or another of the sea. The walls were covered with ships' wheels, fishing nets, and assorted shells. And Vickie was waiting for him, a matching starfish-encrusted hairclip pulling her flowing curls from that delightful face of hers.

"This is nice," Brunelle gestured at the decor. "I've never

been here before."

Vickie stood up from her seat on the bench by the door and grabbed his arm. "I hold a lot of hidden treasures, Dave. If you stick around long enough to find out."

Brunelle took in a deep breath. So much for superficial small talk. It was going to be deep-meaning double entendres. He was a little tired for that kind of conversation. But Vickie looked great. And the smell from the kitchen was absolutely mouth-watering. He could endure it.

"That sounds like good advice," he replied, putting his hand on hers, which was still holding his bicep. "Especially over all-you-can-eat king crab legs."

He'd noticed the promotional sign behind the hostess.

Vickie laughed. "Well, then I'm doubly glad I picked this place."

Brunelle looked around at the not at all ostentatious eatery, seemingly devoid of overly wealthy drug addicts, fueled by authentically good food and word-of-mouth. "Me too."

The hostess led them to a small table by a window. Most of the window was taken up by the nearby condos' parking garage, but there was a peek-a-boo view of Lake Washington between the buildings. Brunelle chose the seat that let Vickie see the water.

The first minutes were taken up by a review of the menu, discussions about food options, waiters bringing water, a couple of jokes about the wooden mallet that accompanied the more traditional knife and fork, and generally avoiding heavier subjects. But that didn't last once the orders were in, and the double entendres proved too cumbersome to maintain.

"I'm glad you texted, Dave," Vickie said over a sip of her white wine. "We didn't get much time to catch up the other night."

Brunelle nodded. "Yeah, that wasn't really my crowd," he

admitted. "Legally or financially."

Vickie nodded. "You never were very comfortable at parties," she recalled.

"Depends on the party," Brunelle responded. "And the people. But that's probably true for most people."

Vickie shrugged. "Maybe. Either way, I'm glad our paths crossed again. Although..." she trailed off.

"Yeah," Brunelle agreed. "This wasn't probably how I would have imagined running into you again. I'm sorry about what's happening. And what happened. The divorce..."

But Vickie waved his concern away. "Don't. The divorce was a long time coming. Whatever craziness has gotten into his head is his problem. It's not mine any more. And not my kids' either. He made his bed; he can lie in it."

Brunelle frowned slightly. "I'm kind of making his bed for him a little."

But Vickie shook her head. "No, it's all his doing. You're just making sure he doesn't get away with it. You didn't put the gun in his hand, you didn't tell him to shoot anybody, especially not some homeless guy in a parking garage at midnight."

"I don't think he was homeless," Brunelle replied, recalling some of the details of the case. "He was scraping by, but he had a stable residence, I'm pretty sure."

"Dave?" Vickie said.

Brunelle cocked his head. "Yeah?"

"Shut up about the case," she instructed. "Shut up about Neil. Talk about us."

"Us." Brunelle nodded. "Yeah, that's a better topic of conversation. I like us."

"What happened to us?" Vickie asked, pulling another sip of wine over her lips. "We were really good together."

Brunelle frowned again. "Maybe too good. It was really intense."

"It was really good," Vickie laughed, deepening her voice at the word 'good.' "I mean, maybe the best I've had. Honestly, I've missed that. A lot."

Brunelle could feel a blush sting his cheeks. But other parts of his body were competing for the rush of blood. "I've missed you too. I never thought I'd see you again. You left for a different world."

"Me?" Vickie laughed. "Our world was rich college kids, drinking, screwing, and avoiding the real world. You're the one who left. You and your criminals and murderers. That's a different world."

Brunelle shrugged. "Maybe. It's a real world, but yeah, one most people probably don't think about. Or want to." He considered for a moment. "Maybe I just wasn't your type."

Vickie smiled and raised an eyebrow. "Oh? And what's my type?"

"Not me," Brunelle answered. "Maybe if I'd gotten a high-powered corporate law job. Maybe if I could have earned more money than just a public servant."

Vickie's smile faded. "Are you calling me a gold digger?"

"No," Brunelle replied immediately. "I'm saying you would expect your partner to be successful, to want to be as successful as you."

Vickie lowered her eyes. "I'm not sure how successful I am, Dave. I have an M.B.A., but I gave up my career when Neil, Jr., was born. Then Emily came, and all of a sudden I've been out of the work force for almost a decade. It didn't matter financially because of Neil's success, but for me personally…"

"For you, it matters," Brunelle understood.

"Yeah," Vickie answered, raising her eyes again to meet Brunelle's.

"So you have another chance to reach for the brass ring," Brunelle encouraged. "If you're the same Victoria Cross I knew back then, you'll grab it with both hands and never let go again."

Vickie sat silently for several moments. "I think I'm that same Victoria Cross," she said. "But it might still be nice to have a partner who helps me grab the brass ring, instead of talking me out of it."

That time, the blood made his heart rush. He raised his own drink. "Here's to new beginnings."

Vickie smiled and clinked her glass to his. "And new partners."

CHAPTER 13

Under the court rules, a party filing a motion had to give the opposing party at least five days' notice before there could be a hearing on the motion. And under the court rules, "five days" excluded weekends, so it was really a full week. Leave it to a lawyer to need two rules to define one week. So one week after Khachaturian's 'Motion to Exclude Expert Testimony' found its way to Brunelle's desk, Brunelle found himself back in Judge Nguyen's courtroom. And he was once again joined by Det. Emory, Beverly and Tom Jenkins, and the esteemed Maxwell Hutchinson.

And a reporter.

Ugh, Brunelle thought, as he saw the camera set up in the back of the courtroom.

"Hey, Jim," he greeted the newsman, knowing him from years of prior contacts. He knew the cameraman too. "Hey, Carl. What are you guys doing here? This is just a preliminary motion about expert testimony. Pretty dry stuff. Figured you guys'd wait until the trial got started for real."

"We got a call," Jim answered. "They said there might be something big happening on the Neil Rappaport case."

Brunelle frowned and looked over at the defense table. Khachaturian was already there, his client seated next to him. No sign of Voegel or Walker, though. Still, Brunelle certainly hadn't called the media, so that left the defense attorney as the most likely suspect. Brunelle knew enough not to care that the reporter was there, but to wonder why the defense would.

He shrugged at the reporters. "I don't know about that. Like I said, just a preliminary motion about some expert testimony on the video. Pretty dry stuff, if you ask me."

He departed and checked in with his other guests. Emory had just come to watch again. Same with the Jenkinses, who seemed more relaxed than at the beginning of the last hearing. Having won that probably lent Brunelle some credibility with them. And then a check-in with Hutchinson.

"Thanks for coming back up," Brunelle said. "I don't think this will take very long, but it's important."

Hutchinson nodded, a bit stiffly. "Am I allowed to talk about my resolution enhancement algorithm? I mean, now that I've been forced to reveal its details to you and the defendant? A defendant, by the way, who has the expertise and assets to steal the ideas and develop his own competing software."

Brunelle considered for a moment. "You can talk about the algorithm." Then he turned and walked to his own table.

He avoided greeting Khachaturian. He might have tried if Rappaport hadn't been there, but it was always awkward to talk with defense attorneys over the head of their clients. Better to focus on the motion and let his arguments do the talking for him.

Nguyen took the bench shortly thereafter and the hearing was off and running.

"Once again, this is your motion, Mr. Khachaturian," the judge explained, "but unlike the previous hearing, you aren't challenging the authenticity of the evidence. You are alleging it should be suppressed under the evidence rules. I think that puts the burden on you, so I will hear first from the defense."

Brunelle was used to going first, but was fine with letting Khachaturian have to frame out the argument for a change. He'd listen to what the defense attorney had to say, then put Hutchinson on the stand to rebut all of it. Easy.

"Thank you, Your Honor," Khachaturian said as he stood up to address the court. "I'll start by conceding that Mr. Hutchinson would, if permitted, identify my client as the person depicted in the video from the Lincoln Properties garage on the night of the murder."

Brunelle looked up from where he'd planned to take quiet notes. And maybe doodle a little during the more boring parts of the hearing.

Khachaturian continued. "The issue is not whether Mr. Hutchinson can or cannot identify the shooter. If permitted to take the stand, he undoubtedly will claim to be able to do so. That is a factual question. But this motion is a legal motion. And the legal issue is not whether he can tell the jury of his identification, but rather whether he should be allowed to do so."

Brunelle nodded slightly. He understood the difference. And undoubtedly so did Judge Nguyen.

"Therefore," Khachaturian said, "we would ask that Mr. Hutchinson be excluded from testifying at today's hearing. His opinion that he can identify someone from a surveillance video is conceded. There is no need for him to say so on the stand."

Brunelle stood up. "The State would object to that, Your Honor. Mr. Hutchinson is present in court today and ready to explain how he was able to identify Mr. Rappaport as the person who murdered Gerald Jenkins."

"His presence is irrelevant, Your Honor," Khachaturian returned. "We did not ask for him to be present, this is our motion, and as I just explained, it is a purely legal motion which the Court can resolve without factual testimony."

"Testimony about his qualifications as an expert," Brunelle interjected.

"Which the Court has already heard, at the last hearing," Khachaturian pointed out.

"Enough," Judge Nguyen interrupted. "This is not going to degenerate into an argument between the parties. All comments will be directed to the bench."

The lawyers nodded and apologized. That was the procedure; it was just easy to get derailed, and some of the judges were happy to watch the train wreck. But not Nguyen.

"Mr. Brunelle," she said, "I will hear from you when it's your turn. Right now, I'm hearing from Mr. Khachaturian." She looked to the defense attorney. "Without agreeing to it, I understand your argument regarding the need, or lack of it, for testimony today. I will decide whether I need to hear from Mr. Hutchinson, after you've completed your argument as to the merits of your motion. So please move on to that, counsel."

"Of course, Your Honor," Khachaturian acquiesced. "Thank you, Your Honor." He took a moment to still his thoughts, then launched into the substance of his argument. Without notes, Brunelle noted with some dismay. He was starting to see why this guy was a Top Litigator.

"Expert testimony," Khachaturian explained calmly, "is governed by the seven-hundred series of the Evidence Rules. ER 702 states unequivocally that 'a witness qualified as an expert' may testify 'in the form of an opinion' *if*," he raised a finger for emphasis, "and *only if* the expert's 'scientific, technical, or other specialized knowledge will assist the trier of fact—the jury—to understand the evidence or to determine a fact in issue.' Here, the expert's specialized knowledge is in how videos are captured and recorded. He is not an expert in identification of human faces. When it comes to looking at an image of a face and saying whether it is or is not a particular person, he is no more of an expert than anyone else in the room, and certainly no more than the jurors, whose decision as to identity will determine the outcome of this case."

Khachaturian paused to take a drink from the small water cup he'd poured himself before the judge took the bench.

"Mr. Hutchinson has an impressive resume, a successful consulting business, and a cache of entertaining war stories of cracking cases in other jurisdictions," Khachaturian allowed. "But that is all the more reason why he shouldn't be allowed to invade the province of the jury and tell them who the person in the video is or is not. They can make that determination for themselves."

Judge Nguyen had narrowed her eyes as Khachaturian spoke. "But doesn't ER 704 state clearly that 'Testimony in the form of an opinion is not objectionable because it embraces the ultimate issue to be decided by the trier of fact'?"

"It does, Your Honor," Khachaturian had to concede—how could he not? The rules were the rules. But the interpretation of those rules—that's where the lawyering came in. "But the ultimate issue in this case will be whether the State has proved beyond a reasonable doubt that Mr. Rappaport murdered Gerald Jenkins. The identification from the video is only one part of that. So it's not truly the ultimate issue, and the Court can suppress it."

Nguyen frowned. "You're saying Mr. Hutchinson could give an opinion as to whether Mr. Rappaport is guilty of murder, but not of whether he's the person in the video?"

Khachaturian gave a body movement halfway between a

shrug and introducing a play and stepping aside for the curtain to open. "If he were qualified to give an opinion about whether Mr. Rappaport committed the murder, then I would suggest that such an opinion would be based on more than just the video. It would be based on all of the evidence, how it fits together, and years of experience solving similar cases. But that's not what he's being asked to do here. What he's being asked to do here is to project two photos on the wall, one a still from the video and the other my client's Department of Licensing photo, and tell the jury that in his expert opinion, it's the same person. But there's nothing expert-like about that opinion. Anyone can make that determination—or not. And the jury should be allowed to do so without undue influence from someone holding himself out to be an expert in other areas."

Nguyen was still frowning, in thought. She waited a moment, then, "Anything further, Mr. Khachaturian?"

"Not at this time," the defense attorney answered, "but I would like an opportunity to respond to whatever arguments Mr. Brunelle might make."

That was standard procedure and Nguyen shrugged it off with an "Of course" before turning to the prosecution table. "Okay, Mr. Brunelle, I will hear from you now. And could you please begin by addressing how Mr. Hutchinson is more qualified than the average juror to recognize a face on a video screen?"

Brunelle stood up and suppressed the flinch Judge Nguyen's question provoked. She was buying Khachaturian's argument, at least in part.

"Of course, Your Honor," Brunelle responded. "This is not a case of direct, eyewitness identification. That is, there wasn't someone in the garage at the time of the shooting, who saw Mr. Rappaport step off the elevator, walk up behind Mr. Jenkins, and shoot him twice through the head."

Brunelle could have just said, 'There wasn't an eyewitness in the garage,' but it was never a bad idea to remind the judge, in the middle of an esoteric legal argument, that there was a real case, with a real murder, and a real victim.

"And I would point out, that in such a case, that witness would be allowed to give his or her opinion as to the identity of the shooter."

"But doesn't that support Mr. Khachaturian's point," Judge Nguyen interrupted, "that suspect identification does not require expertise?"

Brunelle kept a professionally confident half-smile pasted on his face despite the question. "It might support that sub-point, Your Honor," he answered, "but his main point is that no expertise is required for an identification from video. And it is with that point that the State disagrees."

He shifted his weight into a more professorial posture, raising one hand shoulder-height to punctuate his arguments. "The identification in this case—whoever makes it, whether it be Mr. Hutchinson, Detective Emory, or simply the jurors—will be based on viewing a series of two-dimensional digital images. There are limitations in the capture and display of such images. Mr. Hutchinson can speak to how that process works, how real life is translated to two-dimensional pixels, and how it is still a reliable means of identification."

"We aren't arguing it's unreliable," Khachaturian stood to interrupt. "We're arguing the jury should make the determination, not Mr. Hutchinson."

Nguyen shot him a glance. "I thought I told the attorneys not to interrupt. I already told you, you would get to respond to Mr. Brunelle's arguments."

Khachaturian lowered his eyes. "Yes, Your Honor. Sorry,

Your Honor." And he retook his seat.

But the judge looked back to Brunelle and asked, "What about that argument, Mr. Brunelle? If they don't attack the accuracy or reliability of the video, why does Mr. Hutchinson need to tell the jury it's Rappaport they see? Why can't the jury make that determination for themselves? Why shouldn't I *require* them to make that determination by themselves?"

"They will make that determination, Your Honor," Brunelle tried. "But there's no reason Mr. Hutchinson can't give his expert opinion to help them in making that decision."

Judge Nguyen presented a twisted frown as she considered the arguments, and her pending decision. "Mr. Khachaturian? Anything further?"

Brunelle considered reminding the judge that Hutchinson was still present and he still wanted to call him as a witness. But she knew that. And he knew she knew it. No reason to piss her off any more than he might already have—or would as the case progressed. So he sat down again and awaited Khachaturian's rebuttal argument.

It was brief. "Just so the Court clearly understands the issue here," Khachaturian said. "Mr. Hutchinson is not an expert in suspect identification and there is a great danger that the jury would attach undue significance to his personal opinion that the person in the video is my client. Let him explain how video works, let him put those photos on the wall, but don't let him say that he thinks the shooter is Mr. Rappaport. That's for the jury to decide. Otherwise," he finished throwing his arms wide, "why even have juries?"

Judge Nguyen thought for several moments. She leaned back in her chair and tapped a finger on her lips. Then she leaned forward again and began writing on her legal pad. The attorneys—

and everyone else in the courtroom—were left to sit in awkward and anticipating silence. Brunelle could hear the blood in his ears. Emory and Hutchinson were there. The Jenkinses. And the media. And he knew he was about to lose.

"I'm going to grant the defense motion," Nguyen suddenly announced, adding quickly, "in part. I agree with Mr. Khachaturian that Mr. Hutchinson is not an expert in suspect identification. Therefore, he should not be allowed to give his personal opinion as to the identity of the person captured in the video. However, he can explain how the images in the video were captured and explain what features the jury should or shouldn't consider when they make the determination of the identity of the person in the video."

"Thank you, Your Honor," Khachaturian put in.

"I'm not finished, counsel," she warned him, "My ruling is based in part on defense counsel's representation that he will not attack the accuracy or reliability of the video at trial."

"Correct, Your Honor," Khachaturian knew to confirm in order to preserve his win. "We already made that argument, and it was denied. Hence today's motion."

The judge nodded. She looked to Brunelle. "You are free to ask me to reconsider this ruling, Mr. Brunelle, if you believe the defense has indeed attacked the video at trial."

Brunelle nodded. Small comfort. Khachaturian knew not to do that in front of the jury. Not only would it invite Judge Nguyen to change her mind, but really? What jury would think the video wasn't reliable? It wasn't 1950. They'd be upset if there *weren't* a surveillance video. "Yes, Your Honor."

There wasn't anything more to the motion, and Nguyen wasn't going to take any testimony, so the hearing concluded. It was all over but the crying, as they say. Or, in this case, the yelling.

"We lost?" Beverly Jenkins demanded first, before Brunelle

could even get to Hutchinson to apologize for having wasted his time driving up again from Portland.

"Uh, not completely," Brunelle replied. "It probably sounded like that, but it was more like a tie. Our expert can't say the shooter was Rappaport, but they can't say the video isn't accurate. That's not bad."

"It's not good either," Beverly shot back from her scooter.

"Not good enough," her son put in. "The whole case is that video, right? And now the jury don't get to hear that the killer was Rappaport. How are they gonna convict him if no one gets to say it's him in the damn video?"

"It's not no one," Brunelle tried to explain. "I can still argue it. It's just that Mr. Hutchinson can't say it as an expert."

"But you weren't there," Tom pointed out. "You're just the lawyer."

"Yes, well, Mr. Hutchinson wasn't there either," Brunelle replied, a bit too defensively. Then he remembered to pull back. "I'm sorry we didn't get a complete victory here today, but it would be the rare case where either side won every motion. The important thing is, the jury will see the video and they will know—just like I know, and the detective knows, and Hutchinson knows—the shooter is Neil Rappaport. That's what matters."

But the Jenkinses weren't convinced. "To you," Tom grumbled. "Come on, mom. Let's go."

Brunelle frowned as they headed for the exit. Not only had he not placated, he'd violated the underpromise rule by suggesting the jury would definitely identify Rappaport as the shooter. That was suddenly a lot more in question than it had been before Nguyen's ruling.

Hutchinson was next. "So I didn't need to drive all the way up here?" he started with.

"Apparently not," Brunelle shrugged. "I'm sorry. I thought the judge would want to hear from you."

Hutchinson moved on. "And so I can't say the person in the video is the defendant, is that right?" he asked.

"Right," Brunelle confirmed.

"Even with my enhancement software?"

Again, "Right."

"So then," Hutchinson crossed his arms, "why did I have to give over all that information to Rappaport? If I can't even talk about it at trial? Why not just give him the patent to it right now?"

Brunelle sighed. "I have to give over anything I might use. And I think we can still use the software at trial. In fact, we probably need to now. You can enhance the video so the jury will know—even without you saying it—that the person on the video is definitely Rappaport."

Hutchinson didn't seem placated. "Well, next time you think I need to drive to Seattle, maybe you could confirm with the judge first?"

Brunelle managed a pained smile. He couldn't afford to piss off Hutchinson. He and his algorithm had actually become even more important to the case. "Of course, Mr. Hutchinson. And please do accept my apologies. I think she was wrong not to hear from you, but she's the judge."

"Will she be the trial judge too?" Hutchinson asked.

Brunelle nodded. "Yes. At this point, she's made enough rulings, it doesn't make sense to transfer the case to another judge for trial. Not on a murder case."

Hutchinson gave a sardonic smile. "Well, good luck then, Mr. Brunelle. Looks like you're going to need it."

Hutchinson departed then, and Brunelle looked around for Emory. She'd cheer him up. But she'd left already too, without talking to him. The courtroom was empty.

Brunelle sighed again, then packed up his things. He'd have to figure out how this impacted his trial strategy. He had been counting on the Great Maxwell Hutchinson telling the jury Rappaport was guilty. He stepped into the hallway with several possible adjustments swirling in his head, so he let out a startled gasp when Jim called his name and Carl flicked the camera light on in his face.

"Any comment on the judge's ruling, Mr. Brunelle?" Jim asked. "How are you going to show Mr. Rappaport was the murderer if no one can tell the jury that?"

"Uh, that wasn't exactly the judge's ruling…" Brunelle started to explain. His brain was still shifting gears, remembering how to deal with the media on a pending murder case.

"But that's just it, right?" Jim pressed. "Without the I.D., how do you prove the case? I mean, why would a billionaire tech mogul like Neil Rappaport kill a small time drug dealer like Gerald Jenkins?"

Brunelle had regained his wits. He gave the answer he knew to give the media. "Sorry. No comment."

But the real answer echoed silently in his mind: *I don't know.*

CHAPTER 14

The following week, Brunelle was still stinging from Judge Nguyen's ruling, but he also had other work to do, And other cases that needed attention, although The State of Washington v. Neil Rappaport would be his next trial. And to make room for that, he needed to deliver a scheduling order on one of his other cases to the presiding judge. That meant a trip to The Pit, the conference room just off the main day-to-day criminal courtrooms, where a gaggle of defense attorneys and prosecutors spent the day negotiating cases. It was the sausage factory floor for the 95% of criminal cases that settled short of trial. It was also where colleagues from both sides of the aisle shared weekend stories and photos of their kids with lawyers they would know for two or three decades regardless of which side they were on. Hell, their kids might have been on the same baseball team that very Saturday.

Brunelle dropped the scheduling order off with the judge's clerk, then made his way back through The Pit. On his way, he spotted Jessica Edwards, one of the top public defenders in the county and a frequent opponent. And also, in his estimation anyway, a friend.

"Hey, Jess," he greeted her.

She looked up from the police reports she was studying. "Oh, hey, Dave. How's it going? Heard you're in the middle of some high-profile murder case again?"

Brunelle nodded. "Yeah, I guess. It's a weird one. Out of Bellevue. A shooting in a parking garage under one of their high-end retail towers." He sat down in the empty seat next to her. There were a few other attorneys, defense and prosecution, around that particular table, but they were discussing their own cases.

"Yeah," Edwards confirmed. "I heard a little bit about it. It's a small courthouse." She grinned slightly. "I heard you lost a big motion last week."

Brunelle countered her smile with a frown. "It wasn't that big of a motion," he insisted. "And it was more of a draw."

Edwards's grin broadened. "Sure, Dave. That's what you prosecutors always say when you lose."

Brunelle decided not to pursue that line of verbal joust. Instead, he turned to something more interesting to him just then. "The defense attorney is some guy named Eric Khachaturian. I've never met him before. Do you know anything about him?"

Edwards's smile sweetened—in a saccharine way—and she tipped her head toward Brunelle. "You want me to sell out a fellow defense attorney? Come now, Dave. There are rules. He and I are on the same team."

"Aren't we all the team of justice?" Brunelle offered.

Edwards thought for a moment. Then, "No. Of course not. I'm on my client's team. You can claim justice or whatever, but my ethics are for my client and my client only."

"See? Not for other defense attorneys." Brunelle seized on her statement. "So, tell me what you know about him."

Edwards laughed. "Nice try, Mr. Prosecutor. I'll just tell you what anyone else would tell you. He's smart, he's prepared, and he's expensive. But from what I hear, he's worth it. You have your work cut out for you with him."

Brunelle frowned. "Yeah, I'm already seeing that. So, no Achilles' heel?"

"Do I look like Paris to you?" Edwards replied. When Brunelle's brows knitted together, she followed up. "You don't know who Paris is, do you?"

Brunelle shrugged. "A city in France?"

Edwards rolled her eyes. "Well, yes. But it's named after Paris, the Trojan champion who defeated Achilles in the Trojan War."

"Oh, right," Brunelle replied nonchalantly. "*That* Paris. Sure. I knew that. Big wooden horse and all that. Right. So, anyway, any dirt on Khachaturian?"

Edwards shook her head. "Read a book sometime, Dave."

"I will, if I can find the time," he replied. "Maybe if you give me something on Khachaturian I can get this case resolved and I can read all about Achilles and Paris and Berlin and whoever else."

Edwards lowered her head into her hands. "How can you seem so intelligent in court and so not right now?"

"It's part of my charm," Brunelle suggested.

But Edwards wasn't biting. She raised her head again. "He's smart, he's prepared, and..." she paused, looking over Brunelle's shoulder, "he's walking this way right now."

Brunelle spun around to see Khachaturian navigating the obstacle course of attorneys and pulled-out chairs in The Pit, and coming straight for them.

"Mr. Brunelle," he said as he reached their table. "I didn't expect to see you here, but I'm glad I did. Here." He handed Brunelle yet another pleading. "This saves me a trip to your offices."

Brunelle looked down to see what he was holding. It was another motion to suppress. When he looked up again to ask Khachaturian about it, the defense attorney had already waded back into the maze, heading toward the exit.

"What is it?" Edwards asked.

"'Motion to Suppress Fingerprint Evidence,'" Brunelle read aloud. He skimmed the front page for the grounds for suppression. "For lack of scientific reliability under *Frye v. United States*." He looked up at Edwards. "Is he fucking kidding? Fingerprint evidence not scientifically reliable?"

Edwards didn't reply. She took the pleading from Brunelle and skimmed through the interior pages. "Yep, he's citing that study by the National Institute of Standards and Technology from a few years ago. They said fingerprint evidence isn't reliable."

"There's no fucking way they said that," Brunelle countered, snatching the motion back from Edwards.

"Well, they sort of did," Edwards allowed. "They said the collection of them was science, but the comparison wasn't. It's just some forensic technician in the police department saying they match."

"Because they do," Brunelle snapped. It was bad enough he had to defend the technology of video recording. Now he had to defend fingerprinting?

"Maybe," Edwards shrugged. "But a lot of times the recovered fingerprints are only partial prints, or distorted, or smeared, or whatever. The NIST said comparison was more art than science."

Brunelle rubbed a hand over his head, using the other hand to clutch the motion he was trying to stare a hole through.

"Looks like you'll be reading that NIST study this weekend

instead of *The Iliad*, huh?" Edwards asked.

He looked up at her, with the same glare he'd been boring into the pleading. It was a good thing they were friends. "Fuck you, Jess."

CHAPTER 15

Edwards had taken Brunelle's 'fuck you' in the spirit in which it was offered: frustrated, but friendly. She told him not to worry, that no judge in the county was going to suppress fingerprint evidence, and to try and relax. Do something to take his mind off of it, and come back to it later with a fresh attitude.

So rather than making time to read the NIST study that weekend, or *The Iliad*, Brunelle made dinner reservations. In Seattle. Vickie could come to his turf for their second date.

He'd picked a high-end Italian place halfway between Seattle University and the main drag on Capitol Hill. With rustic décor and dim lighting, it had an undeniably romantic atmosphere. And the food was top notch too. But mainly, he was looking for romantic atmosphere. And what might follow.

"What a great place," Vickie commented as they sat down. "I haven't been here in ages."

Brunelle kept his smile from falling. He'd hoped to show the place off to her. It hadn't occurred to him she'd been there before. "Uh, yeah. It's one of my favorite restaurants."

"Very romantic," Vickie observed with a grin. "I like it."

Brunelle kept that smile going despite the ease with which Vickie saw through his plans. He wasn't half as clever as she was. At least the food was good.

Conversation was light, if a little superficial. First dates were exciting, nerve-wracking affairs. Second dates were the true make-or-break situations. They lacked the artificial immediacy of that first date, and the increased level of realism could either launch the relationship forward, or send it crashing and burning. Luckily, the restaurant also served good drinks.

When dinner was done, and they both had a well-crafted cocktail in their systems, it was time to see whether they were going to launch or crash and burn.

"That was nice," Brunelle said as they stood up to leave. "What should we do now?"

"How about a walk?" Vickie suggested. "Don't you live nearby?"

Houston, we have lift off.

"Yeah," Brunelle answered. "My condo's not too far. Well, it kind of is, but it's a nice night for a walk."

They stepped outside and Brunelle turned them toward downtown. Vickie took his arm. It was a nice night indeed.

The freeway was between them and their destination, so they only had a few choices of where to traverse it. Brunelle opted for the one with the better views of Lake Union and the Seattle skyline. The views gave them a chance to talk about nothing much in particular and when they were within a few blocks of Brunelle's place, he pointed out his favorite local bar.

"Should we stop for another drink?" he asked.

"Don't you have anything at your place?" Vickie countered.

"I've got bourbon," Brunelle confirmed. "And glasses. Not sure about ice, though."

"I won't need any ice," Vickie assured. "I like it neat."

Brunelle smiled at the opportunity for a double entendre response. He passed though. They were close. The only thing he could do at that point was screw it up.

Through the lobby, up the elevator, and over his threshold. There was no need for another drink. No opportunity either. As soon as the door closed behind them, the clothes started coming off. A trail of garments from the front door to the bedroom. Jackets, shoes, shirts. Bra, belt, pants.

It had been too long and just the right amount of time. Brunelle looked down at Vickie, laying naked on his bed, her body illuminated by the lights of the city. He didn't ever want to forget how she looked just then. And as she pulled him down onto her, he knew he wouldn't.

CHAPTER 16

Brunelle's thoughts did indeed linger over that night for several days, even as the hearing on the motion to suppress fingerprint evidence approached. He'd made the time to review the NIST study and while it did criticize fingerprint matches as more art than science, he took solace in the fact that, as Edwards had said, there was no judge in the county who was going to say fingerprint evidence wasn't scientifically reliable. He hoped.

Jim and Carl were back, as were the Jenkinses and Emory. But instead of Maxwell Hutchinson, Forensic Technician Daniel O'Rourke of the Bellevue Police Department was the star witness. He looked every bit the desk-jockey fingerprint tech: middle-aged, a little overweight, and scared out of his mind to have to testify. No one challenged fingerprint matches any more. No one except Eric Khachaturian.

"Don't worry," Brunelle tried to calm him in the few minutes they had before Judge Nguyen took the bench. "Just explain how you make a match. The judge will understand. I'm sure she's presided over hundreds of cases with fingerprint evidence."

O'Rourke nodded, but didn't answer audibly.

That's fine, Brunelle thought. *Save your voice.*

As he returned to the prosecution table he looked over at Emory, who gave him an encouraging thumbs up. He avoided looking at the Jenkinses. Not good bedside manner, but he wasn't a doctor. And it wouldn't matter anyway. How they thought of him would depend entirely on the outcome of the hearing.

"All rise!" the bailiff announced as the judge entered the courtroom. Brunelle stood at the prosecution table; Khachaturian was again alone with Rappaport at the defense table. And they were off.

Judge Nguyen likened the hearing to the first attack on the video and put the burden on Brunelle to establish the scientific reliability of the evidence—notwithstanding its admission in courts across the country for a century already. That meant he went first.

"The State calls Daniel O'Rourke to the stand."

O'Rourke made his way from the back of the courtroom and was sworn in by the judge. Brunelle started with name and occupation.

"How long have you been a Forensic Technician with the Bellevue Police Department?"

"Almost twenty-seven years," O'Rourke replied.

"And have you spent that entire time working with fingerprint evidence?" Brunelle asked.

"Yes, sir," O'Rourke answered. "I have other duties as well. Photographing crime scenes, for example. But my main duty is the collection and comparison of fingerprint evidence."

Brunelle nodded encouragingly. "Could you explain how you might come to be asked to compare fingerprint evidence?"

"Yes, sir," O'Rourke repeated. He was still nervous, but like anyone else, he started getting comfortable talking about a topic he knew well. "There are basically two types of fingerprint evidence.

First, there are the fingerprints from a crime scene, which we call 'latent prints' because they just sit there, latent, until and unless someone lifts them. Then, there are confirmed prints, which are those taken by law enforcement from a known individual. Then we compare the latent print to a confirmed print to see if we can identify who left the latent print behind."

"Okay," Brunelle said. "And how long have you personally been doing that?"

"Well, like I said, almost twenty-seven years."

"And how long has law enforcement generally been using fingerprint evidence to identify suspects?"

O'Rourke cocked his head. "You mean, like, ever? How long have police been using fingerprint evidence at all?"

"Yes," Brunelle confirmed. "How long has fingerprint evidence been used by law enforcement in the United States?"

"Uh, well, I'm not sure about the United States," O'Rourke answered, "but everyone who does this work knows about the Francesca Rojas case in Argentina in 1892. She murdered her children and accused a neighbor of doing it for her refusing his advances. The investigator, Juan Vucetich, noticed a bloody thumbprint on the door jamb. He got a fingerprint from Ms. Rojas and it matched. They confronted her and she confessed, saying she'd murdered her children because she wanted to marry her boyfriend, but he didn't like children."

Brunelle smiled. He hadn't heard that story before. The jury was going to love it. "So in that case, it was actually used to exclude the man first accused of the crime?"

"Accused by the actual killer," O'Rourke clarified. "But yes."

"So fingerprint evidence has been used for well over a hundred years to help solve crimes, even serious crimes like murder?"

"Oh, yes," O'Rourke replied, the pride in his voice apparent. "It's a long and noble profession."

"Thank you, Mr. O'Rourke," Brunelle said, ready to end his questioning. But it didn't hurt to remind the judge again. "I should probably ask: did you compare the latent fingerprint from the elevator in this case to the confirmed fingerprint of the defendant at the time he was booked?"

O'Rourke nodded. "I did."

"And did they match?"

"Yes, they did," O'Rourke confirmed.

"Thank you," Brunelle said. "Nothing further."

Khachaturian stood next to cross-examine the witness. O'Rourke actually squirmed a little in his seat. Brunelle would have to work with him on that before the actual trial.

"Hello, Mr. O'Rourke," Khachaturian began. "How are you today?"

O'Rourke paused before answering. "Fine, thank you."

"Good, good," Khachaturian replied. He'd come out from behind the defense table and was sort of pacing in front of the witness stand, looking down at his feet rather than at the witness. "So, part of your job is fingerprinting people, isn't that right? You actually press their fingers down on the pad and roll them and everything?"

O'Rourke nodded. "Yes. We have a digital scanner now, but the process is the same."

"No ink with digital, right?" Khachaturian interjected. "That would ruin the glass, I suppose?"

"Right," O'Rourke answered, relaxing a bit. "We still do some old school, with ink and paper. But most of the time now, we roll the finger across the glass and the computer tells us if it's good enough, or if we have to do it again."

"Oh, so sometimes you have to try more than once?" Khachaturian asked, as if he didn't already know that.

"Sometimes," O'Rourke admitted. "Maybe half the time we have to redo at least one finger."

"And when you fingerprint someone," Khachaturian continued, "you actually take physical hold of their hand and finger and manually roll it across the paper or the glass or whatever, right?"

"Right," O'Rourke answered.

"And you have to tell people to relax their whole arm, right, so you can do it properly?"

O'Rourke nodded. "Yes. A lot of times people tense up at the pressure, or try to roll it themselves, or whatever. We tell them to completely relax their arm and let us do the work."

"And that's because if they're tense, or rolling it wrong, then the computer will say it's not good enough for comparison, right?"

"Right," O'Rourke said.

"And even then," Khachaturian pointed out, "you have to redo at least one finger about half the time?"

"Yes, sir."

"Okay, good, good." Khachaturian continued the absent-minded professor bit. "What about latent prints? Are you there, holding on to someone's arm and rolling their finger just right so they leave a good print for comparison's sake?"

O'Rourke frowned. "No. Of course not."

"Right," Khachaturian said, "and so, often the latent prints have limited or maybe even no comparison value, isn't that right?"

"That is true," O'Rourke conceded. "The first thing we do is determine if the latent has any comparison value. Often they don't."

"And who determines that?" Khachaturian asked.

"I do," O'Rourke answered. "Or one of the other technicians.

That's part of what we do."

"How do you know if it has value?"

O'Rourke thought for a moment. "It depends. There needs to be enough of the print to show at least seven comparison points."

Khachaturian stopped the pacing. "What's a comparison point?"

"Those are the areas on the print that we look at to decide if they match."

"Don't you just overlay them and see if they're the same?" Khachaturian asked. "That's what I've seen on C.S.I."

O'Rourke frowned. "I've seen that too. And it's ridiculous. That would only work if I actually had been there to roll the suspect's finger. That's not how latents are produced. They're left behind when somebody grabs a door handle, or picks up a drinking glass, or presses an elevator button."

"And when they do that," Khachaturian knew, "they might not press their entire finger down, right? Or they might twist their finger a bit, skewing the image, right?"

"Right." O'Rourke nodded. "It's kind of like Silly Putty. You can stretch and warp the image, but every part of the image stays in the same relative position to every other part of the image."

"Or at least," Khachaturian challenged, "you think it does."

"Well, if it doesn't, then it's not a match," O'Rourke defended.

"Is your work reviewed by other fingerprint analysts?" Khachaturian asked.

"Yes," O'Rourke answered. "It's standard practice in the field to have two analysts review every match. The primary analyst makes the match. The secondary analyst confirms it."

"Do secondary analysts ever *not* confirm the primary analyst?" Khachaturian asked.

O'Rourke shifted his weight again. "It does happen sometimes."

"So," Khachaturian put a point on it, "different analysts can look at the same latent, and the same confirmed print, and come to different conclusions?"

"It's uncommon," O'Rourke replied, "but yes. That's why we can be confident when both analysts confirm the match."

"What was the quality of the latent taken from the elevator in this case?" Khachaturian asked.

"It was pretty good actually," O'Rourke answered. "There were nine comparison points clearly visible, and all of them matched."

"Was it distorted at all?"

"A little," O'Rourke conceded, "but not so much that a match couldn't be made."

"But we couldn't put it up on a big screen and overlay them perfectly like on C.S.I.?"

O'Rourke shook his head. "No. You can almost never do that, even with two sets of confirmed prints."

"But," Khachaturian took a softer tone, "you *could* put the latent up on the screen next to the confirmed print, and point out the nine points of comparison, correct?"

"Exactly," O'Rourke agreed. "That would be very helpful, in fact."

"Do you think the jury could really see how they match if you did that?" Khachaturian suggested.

"Oh, yes," O'Rourke answered. "It would be obvious."

"Obvious," Khachaturian repeated. Then, "Thank you, no further questions."

Brunelle opted not to do any redirect-exam. O'Rourke had held up well under cross. There wasn't anything that really needed rehabilitation. Brunelle just wanted to get the hearing over and done with.

"Okay, then," announced Judge Nguyen. "Argument. Mr. Brunelle?"

"Your Honor, I think this motion is similar to the first one brought by defense," he began. "The one to suppress the video for lack of authentication. That expert explained that it's a reliable system or process and the Court ruled it admissible. Similarly, the expert today testified that law enforcement has been using this tool to solve criminal cases—murders even—since 1892. There can't be a legitimate question as to whether fingerprint evidence is admissible at a criminal trial, and if Your Honor were to rule otherwise, you would be the only court in the country to so hold in over a hundred years. We would ask the Court to deny the motion to suppress."

Nguyen frowned slightly at Brunelle's veiled threat. She could see the cameraman in the back of the courtroom too, and she had to run for reelection every four years like every other judge in the state.

She turned to the defense. "Mr. Khachaturian?"

The defense attorney stood up. "Thank you, Your Honor. I would respectfully disagree with Mr. Brunelle. I don't think this motion is like the defense's first motion to suppress the video. Rather, I think it's very similar to the defense's second motion to suppress the expert's specific opinion as to identification."

Brunelle's brows knitted.

"So, if I may, Your Honor," Khachaturian continued, "we would stipulate that fingerprint evidence, generally, meets the standard for admissibility. However, we still maintain that the process of identification is one of personal opinion, and one which the jury can accomplish itself. Officer O'Rourke should be allowed to show the jury the fingerprints in question, and even point out how they are similar, but he should not be allowed to give his opinion as to whether they are a match. In his own words, that much is 'obvious.' And if it's obvious, the jury should be allowed to make that determination unencumbered by the opinion of someone who works for the government, and not just the government, but the police. Thank you."

Brunelle closed his eyes and exhaled through his nose. He managed not to pinch the bridge of his nose. That was a little too much of a tell.

"Any reply, Mr. Brunelle?" the judge asked.

He opened his eyes and pulled out that professional, confident half-smile again. "Yes, Your Honor. I would strongly ask the Court to deny this new motion of the defense. For one thing, I wasn't given notice of this particular motion. The original motion seems to have morphed somehow today, although I wonder if that was entirely by accident. In any event, experts have been able to give their opinions on fingerprint evidence for decades. The Court shouldn't deviate from that established practice now."

"But wasn't that before the report by the National Institute on Standards and Technology?" Judge Nguyen replied. "And wasn't that study commissioned by the United States Department of Justice? So really, isn't the top law enforcement agency in the country saying that we should be very, very careful about the admissibility of fingerprint evidence?"

Brunelle blinked. "I'm not sure we can draw that conclusion, Your Honor. I don't believe the U.S. Attorney's Office has stopped offering fingerprint evidence based on the NIST study."

"And I won't prohibit you from offering that evidence here," Judge Nguyen said. "I agree that it's too well established to suddenly rule it inadmissible. But I do think that NIST was telling courts to be cautious about the opinions of experts regarding whether there's a match. 'More art than science,' they said. So why not have the expert explain the process to the jury and have them decide if there's a match? Wouldn't that avoid the problem raised in the NIST study?"

Brunelle was shell-shocked. "I don't believe it would, Your Honor. No."

"Well, I do," Nguyen replied, looking away from Brunelle. She took a moment to gather her thoughts, then delivered her ruling. "The defense's original motion to suppress the fingerprint evidence in this case for failure to meet the *Frye* standard is denied. However, the defense's additional motion to prevent the fingerprint technician from giving his personal opinion about whether the prints in this case are a match is granted. He may do everything but that final statement."

Are you fucking kidding me? is what Brunelle wanted to say. Instead, he said nothing at all, trying to assess how damaging the ruling would be. If it really was that obvious… But no, there was a difference between a police officer saying fingerprints matched and leaving it up to twelve people who, in order to be seated on the jury in the first place, would likely have absolutely no experience in law enforcement.

Nguyen departed the bench, and Brunelle sat down at the counsel table. He decided to sit there as long as it took for everyone to leave the courtroom. There was no way he was going to talk to the media, and he supposed Emory had already slipped out again, her confidence in him hemorrhaging. Then he remembered O'Rourke and he remembered he should tell him he was free to go. And he supposed he had to say something to the Jenkinses, even if it was just, 'Sorry.'

But when he stood up and turned around, the courtroom was empty. They had all left without talking to him.

He sat down again and lowered his head in his hands. He had definitely forgotten all about his night with Vickie.

CHAPTER 17

Brunelle was at the office early the next morning. But not as early as Duncan.

"Hey, Dave," Duncan said, darkening his doorway well before any of the other staff would arrive. "You got a minute?"

Brunelle knew the answer. And he knew that minute would be in Duncan's office. He followed his boss down the hall.

"I heard the Rappaport case is going a little rocky," Duncan started after they'd sat down on opposite sides of his desk.

Brunelle shrugged. "I wouldn't say that exactly."

"Well, the victim's family would," Duncan answered. "They called to complain about your performance. They said you're losing all the motions and they're afraid the defendant is going to get away with the murder of their loved one."

His tone wasn't exactly stern. Duncan didn't do stern. But it was direct, and honest.

Brunelle's was perhaps a bit less so. "I didn't lose exactly," he insisted. "The judge just limited the evidence a little."

"Your fingerprint expert can't tell the jury that the fingerprint matches Rappaport," Duncan pointed out. "That's not a little limitation."

"Look, the expert can point out all the similarities, he just can't use the word match," Brunelle tried. "And remember, it's all on video."

"And your video expert can't say it's Rappaport either," Duncan countered. "Can anyone say it was him?"

"I can," Brunelle said with a wry grin.

"That doesn't count." Duncan didn't appreciate the quip. "The judge is going to tell the jurors very specifically that the arguments of the attorneys are not evidence. We've all memorized that instruction."

"I know," Brunelle conceded. "I'm not sure why Nguyen is being so careful. But it won't matter. It's him on the video. It's his fingerprint in the elevator. He did it, and I'll prove it."

Duncan let out a long exhale and looked out the window. "You were right, Dave. The media is loving this case. Everyone wants to see the rich guy taken down. And there's nothing more righteous than taking down a murderer. But it was already a thin case, and it's getting thinner. Are you sure you've got this?"

"I've got this," Brunelle assured his boss.

"Do you want to reconsider not having a second chair?" Duncan suggested. "Sometimes co-counsel can help you see things you miss, think of arguments you didn't think of, find case law you might have overlooked..."

Brunelle shook his head. "I've got this," he repeated. "Khachaturian thinks he's winning, but all he's doing is exposing how strong my case is. The jury will get it and I'll make sure they do. I don't need an expert to tell the jury the sky is blue, and I won't need one to tell them it's his ugly mug on that surveillance video or his nine-matching-points-of-comparison fingerprint on the elevator button."

Duncan thought for several moments, then surrendered a tentative nod. "Okay, then. I'll trust you. But damn it, Dave, one more setback and I'll choose your co-counsel myself. Two more, and your co-counsel will be trying it without you. Understood?"

Brunelle appreciated the second chance. The last thing he wanted to do was disappoint Matt Duncan. "Understood."

CHAPTER 18

Brunelle stayed late that night, and then several nights after that. He made general plans to see Vickie that weekend, but the specifics were on hold until Brunelle saw how much work he'd done on the case, and how much of the weekend he'd need to keep working on it. Friday night, he left work a little earlier and stopped by that bar near his condo for a drink before turning in for the night, and the week. He was seated at the bar, about halfway through his first Manhattan, when he decided to text Vickie and confirm they could grab dinner the next night. Maybe there was a show or something they could catch too. It shouldn't always just be dinner and sex. Although…

"David Brunelle?" a voice came from behind him.

Brunelle turned around to face the man who'd just said his name. He didn't recognize the man. Or the two men standing behind him. The speaker was tall—very tall—and solidly built, his muscles apparent through his tightly fitting black sweater. He had shortly cropped blond hair and the slightest trace of an accent, even in those two words.

"That's me," Brunelle confirmed. He never liked being

confronted by strangers. He'd spent his career putting people in prison. Most of them were going to get out again at some point, and he'd been doing it long enough that the car thieves, residential burglars, and armed robbers he'd cut his teeth on as a junior D.A. were undoubtedly free again. And there was no way he could remember everyone he'd prosecuted. For all Brunelle knew, tall, blond, and fearsome had been plotting his revenge for a decade. "Do I know you?"

"No," the man answered, to Brunelle's relief, "but you know Victoria Rappaport."

Brunelle frowned. He set his drink down and turned completely to face the man. He didn't get off the bar stool though. That would just have confirmed he was several inches shorter. "I believe it's Vickie Cross again," he corrected. "And I don't see what business it is of yours."

"It is my business," the man said, "because I am her boyfriend. I am asking you politely to stay away from her."

Brunelle raised an eyebrow. "I doubt you're her boyfriend. She's only been divorced for a couple of months now."

"And she knew she was going to be divorced for three months prior to that," the man replied in that accent Brunelle couldn't place. "We have known each other for a very long time. I am asking you not to interfere."

Brunelle sized up the situation. Large man in front of him. Backed up by two other, not so small themselves, men. Half a drink in his bloodstream. And Vickie on his mind.

He stood up. Yep, several inches shorter. But it didn't matter.

"Fuck you," he said, jabbing a finger at the accented stranger. "And fuck your friends. I don't know who you are, and I don't care. There's nothing, absolutely nothing, that will scare me away from Vickie."

The man took several moments to consider Brunelle's words. Then he took a step back and pointed at him. "You have been warned." Then he and his friends left the bar.

Brunelle stood there for several more seconds, letting the adrenaline begin to subside. Then he returned to his stool. And his drink. And his phone.

Can I see you tonight?

CHAPTER 19

"Motion to Disqualify the Prosecutor," Brunelle read the caption to Khachaturian's latest motion, "for Conflict of Interest."

Nicole had handed it to him as he walked into work Monday morning. "It arrived by fax at 7:30 this morning," she said. "And a process server was waiting with the hard copy at 8:30 when the office opened. You better read it."

"I'm trying," Brunelle replied. He hadn't made it past Nicole's desk; she'd grabbed him on his way past.

"Top of page two," Nicole directed him. "First full paragraph."

Brunelle frowned at her, then turned to the indicated passage. He felt the blood drain from his face.

"The defense has learned that the assigned Assistant District Attorney, David Brunelle, has an irreconcilable conflict of interest in the prosecution of this case, to wit: he has recently entered into a romantic relationship with the defendant's ex-wife and therefore has a personal interest in the outcome of the litigation."

He exhaled deeply. "Fuck."

"Oh, no, David," Nicole scolded. "That's what got you into

this mess in the first place."

But Brunelle tried to play it off. "This is just part of the game, Nicole," he assured her. "Vickie's not a witness. And their divorce was final before the murder."

Nicole raised an eyebrow. "Vickie?" she repeated.

"Yes, Vickie," Brunelle answered with a groan. "I knew her a long time ago. We dated for a short time. I ran into her again because of this case, and we're just catching up. It's perfectly innocent."

Nicole's other eyebrow raised. "Perfectly innocent? Oh, please. I know you, Dave Brunelle. If you're still seeing her, it moved past innocent some time ago."

Brunelle smiled at that. "Thanks for the lecture, Ms. Richards, but I can handle things myself." He shook the pleading bravely. "I'll take care of this."

"Like you took care of the video and the fingerprints?" Nicole jabbed.

Brunelle cocked his head and frowned. "Hey now…"

"Don't 'Hey now' me," Nicole interrupted. "Don't fuck this case up just because you can't keep it in your pants."

Brunelle's frown deepened. "Did it ever occur to you that this might have to do with my heart, not my pants?"

Nicole crossed her arms and thought for a moment. "No."

"Great," Brunelle replied. "Glad you have such a high opinion of me." He turned and headed down the hall toward his office. "Don't worry. Like I said, I'll handle this myself."

Then he walked right past his office and into Duncan's.

"Hey, boss," he started, as Duncan looked up at him. "About that second chair…"

CHAPTER 20

"Me?" Gwen Carlisle put a flattered hand to her chest after Brunelle came to her office to give her the news. Brunelle noticed she'd cut her thick blonde hair a little closer to her jawline. It suited her, he thought.

"You're choosing little ol' me," she went on, "to second-chair another murder case with you? Why, Mr. Brunelle, if I didn't know better, I'd think you were sweet on me."

"Duncan chose you," Brunelle explained. "And I think it's precisely because he's afraid I'd end up sweet on anyone else."

"So, you're not sweet on me?" Carlisle feigned being hurt.

"I'm not really your type," Brunelle replied. "What with my penis and all."

Carlisle laughed. "Well, you're right about that. And it's hilarious when you say 'penis.' Say 'dick' like everyone else. Or 'cock,' or—"

"Okay, can we stop with that?" Brunelle interrupted. "It took me two hours to convince Duncan I could stay on the case. And even then he handpicked my co-counsel. He wanted someone he knew could put up with me and he knew wouldn't end up in bed with me. He's not happy about me dating the defendant's ex-wife."

Carlisle burst out laughing. "You're fucking the murderer's wife? Awesome."

"Ex-wife," Brunelle corrected. "And we're dating."

"You're fucking," Carlisle repeated.

Brunelle sighed. "Yes. Wow, maybe this wasn't a good idea. I could hand the case off to Fletcher..."

"He'd fuck it up," Carlisle said.

Brunelle nodded. "Maybe Yamata. She's ready to try one on her own."

"Are you ready to give this one up?"

Brunelle thought for a moment and shook his head. "No. This is a really bad one. Super-rich guy with everything going for him snuffs out some low-level, barely-scraping-by guy for no apparent reason. I think it was just sport. To see if he could get away with it."

"Is that your motive?" Carlisle asked. "He wanted to see if he could get away with it? Hmm, very Raskolnikov."

"Who?"

"Raskolnikov?" Carlisle repeated. "*Crime and Punishment*? Dostoevsky. God, do you ever read anything?"

"I read the motion to disqualify me," Brunelle answered and he tossed it on her desk. "But you have to write the reply. Boss's orders."

"Great," Carlisle shook her head. "So you bring me onto a case, but my first assignment is to write a brief about why you shouldn't be kicked off?"

"Exactly. Welcome aboard."

"And fuck you too," Carlisle responded. Then she smiled.

"Thanks. All kidding aside, I do appreciate the opportunity."

Brunelle nodded. "And all kidding aside, I appreciate the help."

CHAPTER 21

. .

The second date wasn't the hardest. It was the last date.

Vickie wasn't available the next Friday night, so they made plans for Saturday afternoon. The sooner the better.

She knew something was wrong as soon as she saw him.

"What's wrong, Dave?" she asked.

He was sitting on a bench in the small park just north of the waterfront. It was a beautiful location for a walk, either to the south along the shops and tourist traps, or further north along the rocky beach preserved by the Parks Department before hitting the warehouses of the Interbay District.

He looked up at her, frowning. If he wasn't in front of a jury, he wasn't very good at hiding his feelings. It was too much work, and there was rarely a good reason—not in the long run, anyway. "We need to talk."

"Shit." She kicked at the ground. "Really? Already? Damn it, Dave, I thought we'd last a little longer at least. What's the problem this time? You don't like how I chew my food? Are my nails too long? Too short? You don't like the presets on my car radio? What?"

Brunelle grimaced. "No, it's nothing like that. It's just..." He tried to figure out how best to explain. "Do you know some tall blond guy with an accent?"

Vickie's brow creased for a moment. "Do you mean Mathias?"

"I don't know who I mean," Brunelle answered. "He didn't give me his name. He just said he was your boyfriend. So that was kind of awkward. Especially when he sort of vaguely threatened me."

"He's not my boyfriend," Vickie answered. "He's just a friend."

"You might want to explain that to him then," Brunelle said. "He seemed pretty sure about it."

"He *wants* to be my boyfriend," Vickie elaborated. "I could tell that, even before things turned bad between Neil and me. But we've never dated. He's just a friend I can talk to."

"Or he's a stalker," Brunelle responded. "With stalker friends who stood behind him menacingly while he assured me he was your boyfriend."

Vickie sighed. "Look, this is just a misunderstanding. I'm not dating anyone else. Okay?"

Brunelle's frown weakened, but remained. "Okay. That's good. But still," he looked away, "I think maybe we should take a break anyway. I mean, the trial is coming up and I don't know what's going to happen…"

"So you're afraid of Neil?" Vickie interrupted. "Is that it?"

Brunelle straightened up a bit. "I'm not afraid of Neil."

"I don't know, Dave," Vickie huffed. "Sure sounds like you're scared of someone. Matthias. Or Neil. Or maybe it's me. Maybe you can't handle a woman like me."

He very much wanted to handle a woman like her. But it was complicated. He said as much—at least the last part.

"Complicated?" Vickie scoffed. "What's complicated? Either you like me, or you don't. Either you want to be with me, or you don't. Either you're willing to fight for me, or you're not."

"Now, see," Brunelle raised a finger. "That fighting for you thing. I'm confused. Why would I have to fight against Matthias if he's just a stalker or Neil if he's just your ex? Or is there more to it? Something else I don't know?"

"What didn't you know before?" Vickie demanded.

Brunelle shrugged. "I didn't know about Matthias."

"He's not my boyfriend!" Vickie shouted. "Why would I tell you about him?"

"Why wouldn't you?" Brunelle countered.

"So you think I'm lying to you?" Vickie asked, incredulous.

"Are you?" Brunelle asked.

Vickie didn't answer. She just stared at him, anger flashing beneath the growing glisten. "I guess I misjudged you, Dave. I really did." She looked down and shook her head, laughing darkly to herself. "I should have known better. I should have remembered how you were in college. But I thought you'd grown up. I thought you were brave. Prosecutors are the good guys, right? And good guys are supposed to be brave. But not you, Dave. You're not brave. You're just… you're just *you*."

He thought for a moment. "I don't know how to be anybody else."

"And I guess you never will." Vickie shook her head again, but her eyes were drying. "It's too bad, Dave. We could have been good together. Really good. But now… Well, I guess you'll never know what you missed."

She turned and walked away then, the hurried gait of a hurt lover.

He watched after her. "Oh, I know."

CHAPTER 22

"Did you take care of it?" Carlisle asked the next Monday as they met to walk down to Judge Nguyen's courtroom again.

Brunelle nodded. "Yeah. But I messed it up. It didn't go like I'd planned. But yeah, it's done."

"I figured you'd fuck it up," Carlisle answered. "But I figured it'd get done too."

Brunelle stopped walking and looked at her. "You thought I'd screw it up?"

"Of course," she answered, also stopping in the hallway leading from the elevators. "You're terrible at that sort of stuff. You hide your feelings behind deflection and blame. What'd you say, you didn't like the presets on her car radio?"

Brunelle blinked at her. "No," he said. "I just said we should take a break."

"A break?" Carlisle repeated. "That's pretty cliché, Dave. It's code for 'We should break up but I'm too much of a coward to say so.'"

"Well, that's not all I said," Brunelle defended.

But Carlisle grimaced. "You probably should have just said

that. Whatever else you said, I'm sure it just made it worse."

"Why?"

"Because, Dave," Carlisle shook her head at him, "you suck at this stuff. I just told you that. Duh."

Brunelle was at a loss for words. "Did I mention I'm really glad you're on the case with me?"

"Yeah," Carlisle answered.

"I take it back," Brunelle said. And he walked past her toward Nguyen's courtroom.

* * *

There were several reporters this time, not just Jim and Carl. Two other cameramen, plus a print reporter with a notepad. God bless him and his dying industry. Emory was there too, and stood up to greet them when they walked in. The Jenkinses saw them too, but looked away again, waiting for the judge. Rappaport was at the defense table, flanked by all three of his attorneys.

"Hey, Dave," Emory said as she reached them. "Sorry I had to run after the last hearing. I got called in to interrogate an armed robbery suspect. It was worth it. He confessed to a string of them on the Eastside. He'll be going away for a long time."

"No worries," Brunelle responded. "And good job getting the confessions."

Emory grinned. "I told you I was good at reading people. He just wanted someone to listen to his sob story. 'I lost everything. Boo hoo.' Easy." Then she looked to Carlisle and extended a hand. "Casey Emory. I'm a detective with Bellevue P.D."

"Gwen Carlisle," she introduced herself as she shook the detective's hand. "They brought me on to pull Dave's ass out of the fire."

Brunelle just shook his head.

"Good luck with that," Emory said. But before she could pile on, the bailiff announced the entrance of Judge Nguyen.

Brunelle and Carlisle hurried to the prosecution table as Nguyen asked if the parties were ready to proceed on the defense motion to disqualify Brunelle from the case.

As usual, the prosecution responded first, but Brunelle stayed seated as Carlisle stood to address the judge. "The State is ready. Gwen Carlisle on behalf of the State."

Nguyen nodded to her. "Welcome. Ms. Carlisle. I've read your brief. It's nice to put a face to the name." She turned to the defense table.

A bit to Brunelle's surprise, Khachaturian remained seated and Lisa Walker stood up. "The defense is ready, Your Honor."

"All right then," Nguyen said. She seemed perturbed to have to be presiding over such a sordid motion. Videos and fingerprints were one thing. The romantic life of the lawyers was quite another. "This is the defense motion, so I'll hear first from Ms. Walker."

"Actually, Your Honor," Carlisle interrupted. "If I might, I have some new information which might affect Ms. Walker's argument, and I would hate to save it until I speak and not give her the chance to address it."

Nguyen frowned but looked at Walker. "Do you want to hear this new information before you make your argument, Ms. Walker?"

Walker took a moment to huddle with her teammates, including Rappaport, then looked back up to the judge. "Yes, Your Honor. But just the information; there should be no argument from the prosecutor.

"Agreed," Carlisle offered.

Judge Nguyen nodded to her. "All right then. What's this new information?"

Carlisle cleared her throat. "As the briefing explains, Mr. Brunelle was acquainted with the defendant's now ex-wife back when they were both in college and before she married Mr. Rappaport. This case brought them back in touch, but as of today, there is no romantic relationship between Mr. Brunelle and Mr. Rappaport's ex-wife. Whatever relationship may have existed prior to today's hearing, it is over now."

Judge Nguyen nodded slightly at the information. It wasn't entirely irrelevant, and probably useful to know at the outset. "Anything else?" she asked.

Carlisle thought for a moment. "Just that the State has no intention of calling her as a witness. She has no information relevant to the accusations in this case."

"Okay." Judge Nguyen thanked Carlisle and turned again to the defense table. "Ms. Walker, you may begin whenever you're ready."

The defense attorney hesitated, crouching over to whisper with the other attorneys and her client. After a few more moments, she stood up again. "Did the prosecutor just say they have no intention of calling Ms. Cross-Rappaport as a witness?"

Carlisle looked to Brunelle for confirmation, who gave it in the form of a quick nod. "That's correct, Your Honor. As I understand it, Ms. Cross—or Cross-Rappaport or whatever she goes by now—was not a witness to the crime and had been estranged from the defendant for some time prior to the incident. The State has no plans to call her in its case-in-chief."

Rappaport motioned for Walker to lean over again and he whispered something in her ear. Walker straightened up again. "And the relationship is over?" she asked.

"Yes," Carlisle answered. Still, she looked at Brunelle, who nodded again. "Yes," she repeated.

Another whispered huddle of the defense team, this time with Khachaturian seeming the most animated. After some time, Judge Nguyen interrupted, "Ms. Walker? Are you ready to proceed?"

Walker finished listening to whatever Khachaturian was saying, then turned to address the court. "Your Honor, if the prosecution is willing to enter into a written stipulation that they will not be calling Ms. Cross-Rappaport in their case-in-chief, then the defense will withdraw its motion to disqualify Mr. Brunelle."

Nguyen's eyebrows shot up. Brunelle's did too. Carlisle raised one askance at Brunelle. For the third time, he nodded.

"We can do that," Carlisle answered, half to the court, half to Walker.

"Then the defense withdraws its motion," Walker confirmed. "Our concern was a situation where Mr. Brunelle would be calling Mr. Rappaport's ex-wife as some kind of bad character witness, all the while dating her. It appears that is no longer a concern."

Judge Nguyen hesitated, but she'd spent her career as a judge, and the best judges knew they were the referees, not the players. "All right, then. The defense has withdrawn its motion. There's no longer a need for a hearing."

Then she raised a hand, "But since the parties are both here, I'd like to inquire as to whether this matter will be ready to proceed to trial in two weeks as scheduled?"

Carlisle looked to Brunelle. A fourth nod. "Yes, Your Honor," Carlisle reported. "The State is ready."

All eyes turned to Walker. But Khachaturian stood up to answer the court's question. "The defense will be ready as well, Your Honor. We have no additional preliminary motions. We are ready to prove Mr. Rappaport's innocence."

Brunelle rolled his eyes. Nice soundbite for the cameras, but they both knew that wasn't how it worked. Brunelle and Carlisle would have to prove his guilt. Beyond a reasonable doubt. With no motive.

Nguyen nodded. "Very well, then. I will see all of you back in two weeks, ready to begin trial."

The bailiff banged the gavel and the judge departed the courtroom.

"That was easy," Carlisle whispered to Brunelle as he stood up next to her. "You're welcome."

"Yeah, thanks," he answered. "And you're right. Almost too easy."

CHAPTER 23

The next two weeks went by relatively quickly. With no more motions from Khachaturian, Brunelle and Carlisle were able to focus on the final aspects of their trial preparation: divvying up witnesses, preparing exhibits, and still trying to brainstorm any reasons why Neil Rappaport would want to kill Gerald Jenkins. Even after fourteen days, picking the jury, and finishing all the preliminary motions, the best they could come up with was either: (a) just for sport, or (b) to silence Jenkins for some unknown drug, sex, or other indiscretion. But without evidence of the unknown indiscretion, they would never be allowed to argue it to the jury. And killing someone just for sport didn't seem likely either.

Brunelle decided to do the opening himself, not Carlisle. Opening statement was when you told the jury what you thought the evidence would show. He wasn't going to make Carlisle stand up there and tell the jury they weren't exactly sure what happened—or at least why it happened. He should do that himself. And he figured he'd come up with something by the time they actually got to opening statements.

But twelve hours before he was going to walk into Judge

Nguyen's courtroom to deliver that opening statement, he still hadn't thought of anything. He'd have to hope something would come up during the course of the trial, in time for Carlisle's closing argument. He didn't need the motive, but he sure as hell wanted it.

Speaking of things he didn't need but still wanted, Brunelle hadn't had any contact with Vickie since his poorly executed effort to call a break at the waterfront park. That allowed him to conduct his standard night-before-opening-statement ritual: a glass of bourbon, a balcony, and his own thoughts. The only distraction was the lack of distractions.

Until he was distracted by the buzz of the intercom. Someone was downstairs at the front door. He pushed up from his seat on the balcony, with its view of the other buildings in his neighborhood, and headed back inside to his front door. He pressed the button on the intercom. "Hello?"

"Dave?" came the voice on the other end. "It's Paul." A pause. "Paul Cross."

Brunelle exhaled, not sure what to expect. But he knew what to do. Paul was still an old friend. He pressed the button to unlock the lobby door. "Come on up."

A few minutes later, he was opening his condo door to Paul Cross, his old college friend, and the brother of the woman he just dumped. He wondered which person had come to pay him a visit.

He didn't have to wonder long.

After being polite enough to thank Brunelle for opening the door to him, Paul got right to business. "What the hell is wrong with you, Dave?" he demanded. "I told you she was fragile. I told you not to hurt her. What were you thinking? Or is that it, you just weren't thinking?"

Brunelle put his hands up defensively. "Look, Paul. It's complicated. I don't really want to get into it right now."

"Well, that's too bad," Paul replied. "Because I'm here now. And I want answers."

"You're her brother Paul," Brunelle replied. "Not her dad, not her ex-husband, not her lawyer. I don't think I have to answer to you."

"I'm also your friend," Paul said. "Or I thought we were friends. And either way, I'm still Vickie's brother. I care about her, and I thought you did too. But you hurt her, Dave. You really hurt her. And I want to know why."

"Come on, Paul," Brunelle tried to calm him down. "I have to give opening statement tomorrow in Neil's case. I don't think it's a good idea if I spend tonight arguing about my personal relationships with someone who is clearly upset with me. I need to be able to focus. I need to be able to get some sleep. I can talk to you more about this after the trial. I can talk to Vickie more about this after the trial. But tonight, I don't need this."

"Of course!" Paul threw his hands up in the air. "I don't know why I'm surprised. Of course you won't talk to me. You always were a coward."

"Coward?" Brunelle replied indignantly. "I don't think you need to be casting aspersions at me, Paul. There's more going on than you know, or need to know. So maybe back off the personal attacks, huh?"

But Paul wasn't about to be deterred. "No, Dave, you're a coward. You always were. That's why you took off on Vickie in the first place. And that's why you've never made anything out of your life."

Brunelle crossed his arms. "I think that's a bit of a stretch," he defended. "I've done okay."

But Paul just laughed. "Really?" He gestured at Brunelle's condo. "You live in a two-bedroom apartment. I have pool houses bigger than this. All because I had the courage to take a chance, while you took the easy way out, and grabbed a government job with low hours and a pension."

Brunelle crossed his arms. "I put murderers behind bars. That takes some guts. More guts than putting some app on somebody's phone so they can download some other app."

"That's not why you ended up at the prosecutor's office," Paul shot back. "You went to law school because it was safe. You took a government job because it was safe. I took a risk. I risked everything. And it paid off. That's why I'm successful. And that's why you'll never be. "

He shook his head. "You know, I was going to offer you a cushy job as corporate counsel once I got control of the company. Corner office, time-share in Hawaii, the whole bit. But never mind. Now I see who you really are." He sneered at his old pal. "I should thank you for showing me who you really are. Vicky too. She's lucky. You don't deserve her. She deserves somebody who has the guts to take risks, who has the guts to succeed."

Brunelle had been drinking, and he wondered if maybe Paul had too. Things were bad enough; he didn't want to make them worse. But he was also starting to get pissed off. "I think you should go," he said.

But Paul shook his head. "Not until I've said what I came to say. You stay the fuck away from Vickie, got it? I don't ever want to see you come back into her life. She deserves the best. And you? You're nothing."

Brunelle thought for a few seconds, then pulled his cell phone out of his pocket. "So you make apps for phones?" he confirmed. "How much does that app cost, like $2.99, maybe? And you'd charge more if you could. So, that means you provide something that most people value less than their daily cup of coffee.

It's just that there are a lot of people who want it. There's no depth to your support, just breadth. So you got rich because a lot of people are willing to spend just a little bit for the small convenience that you offer them."

Brunelle sneered. "And so you get a big house, with big pool houses, and more cars than you can possibly drive. Gerald Jenkins gets found dead in a black Audi sedan and everyone thinks he stole it. You probably don't even drive your black Audi sedan. It just sits in your driveway, just another trophy. That doesn't help anyone."

He shook his head at his friend.

"But I do. I help people. I try maybe three or four cases a year. So, take my annual salary and divide it by 3 or 4, and you know what? That's tens and tens of thousands of dollars that I get paid to do what I do. That means what I do is literally thousands of times more valuable than what you do. So fuck you and your mansion, and fuck you and your pools, and fuck you and your cars. I'm happy with my condo, I'm happy with my job, and I'm happy with my life."

He stepped past Paul, and opened his front door again. "And speaking of my condo, get the hell out of it."

Paul narrowed his eyes at Brunelle. "Gladly," he said. "I don't hang around losers like you."

"No," Brunelle replied. "You hang around murderers like Neil Rappaport. Get out."

Paul stormed out and Brunelle closed the door behind him. Then he leaned against the door, closed his eyes, and shook his head.

Opening statements were the next morning. What he needed was to be able to focus, and get a good night's sleep.

"Fuck."

CHAPTER 24

Brunelle didn't sleep well that night. He didn't lie awake all night or anything, but the sleep was fitful. His dreams were coated with past romance and impending court. When the alarm went off, he felt almost less rested than when he'd gone to bed. But he got up, showered, and put on the uniform for opening statement: his best dark suit, his brightest white shirt, and his most power-y red power tie.

But when he walked into court, Carlisle took one look at him and said, "God, you look like hell."

Brunelle's face fell. "Wow. Thanks, partner. Just what I wanted to hear before I give my opening."

Carlisle shrugged. "I call 'em like I see 'em. And I'm seeing someone who looks like he hasn't slept in a few days." She grinned. "What's the matter, tiger? Still get nervous before trial?"

Of course he still got nervous before trial. It was a big deal. Someone was dead. Someone else was facing decades in prison. Friends and relatives and cops and bosses were counting on him. Just like every other trial. And he still got nervous, at least a little bit, before all of them. "No." He shrugged. "Just had a lot on my mind last night."

He turned to scan the gallery. It was fuller than it had been at the pretrial hearings, or would be again until closing argument. Openings and closings were interesting to watch. Witness examination, not so much. Emory was there. And the Jenkinses. Two camera crews in the back. And a collection of younger prosecutors and defense attorneys Brunelle recognized from around the courthouse. There were also several young men and women in dark suits sitting stoically behind Rappaport's table. Associate attorneys from Voegel, Oldman, Khachaturian, and Whoever, come to watch the big dogs.

Det. Emory got up from her seat and made her way down to the prosecution table to wish them good luck.

She nodded approvingly at his suit. "You look great," she assured him, apparently unable to read either his mood or Carlisle's lips. "Knock 'em dead," she said. "So to speak."

"Thanks," Brunelle replied. But he didn't have time to say anything more. Judge Nguyen entered the courtroom and everyone scurried to their places at the bailiff's call to order.

As soon as she sat down, Judge Nguyen looked to the lawyers. "Are the parties ready for opening statements?"

Brunelle stood up first. "Yes, Your Honor."

He was followed by Voegel—not Khachaturian—who also answered, "Yes, Your Honor."

As the bailiff fetched the jury and led them into the jury box, Brunelle wondered if that meant Voegel might try to give the opening. Or maybe he was just showing off for the newbies from his firm. It could make a big difference. Khachaturian was an experienced and, Brunelle had discovered, effective criminal defense attorney. Voegel was a dried up, corporate hack who probably hadn't tried a case in over a decade, and even then it was probably a bench trial about a cracked sewer line or something.

On the other hand, it didn't make any difference. He had his own job to do.

"Ladies and gentlemen," Judge Nguyen said after wishing the jurors a good morning, "please give your attention to Mr. Brunelle who will now deliver the opening statement on behalf of the State of Washington."

The courtroom went silent as Brunelle stepped around his counsel table and took a position directly in front of the jurors. There was something special about the moment before a prosecutor gave opening statement. When the prospective jurors first entered the courtroom for jury selection, they were advised it was a criminal case, and they all looked around to see if they could figure out who the criminal was. Then they wondered what he'd done—not whether he'd done it. When the judge advised them of the charge— murder!—they wondered who he'd killed, and how. And why. When the lawyers asked questions, they weren't allowed to mention the specific facts of the case, but the different theories of the case were suggested by the questions posed.

So, by the time Brunelle stood up to give his opening, the jurors knew it was a criminal case, they knew it was a murder, and they were starting to guess what the lawyers thought might be important in a prospective juror. The one thing they didn't know was the thing every single one of them wanted to know at the beginning: What happened? And finally, someone was going to tell them. Brunelle was going to tell them.

He took one more moment to make sure everyone in the courtroom was waiting on him. Then he began.

"I don't know who that is," he started. The seemingly incongruous quote was followed by its explanation. "That's what the defendant, Neil Rappaport, said when the police told him the name of the man he'd murdered."

They were going with Option A. Murder for sport. They didn't have anything else.

"That's how callous, how removed, how entitled the defendant had become over the years of his unimaginable financial success. Lording over the rest of us, from behind the gated walls of his waterfront compound. He'd conquered the tech industry. He was richer than some countries. He was untouchable."

Brunelle paused. "Or was he?"

He was laying it on a bit thick, but if he was going to sell Option A, he really had to sell it.

"Could he really get away with anything? Had he truly gained that transcendent level of success?" He paused, before answering his own question. "There was only one way to find out. Do the worst thing imaginable, to the lowest person he could find, and see if anyone cared enough to do anything about it."

He paused again and took a step to the side, opening his body to the gallery behind the counsel tables, behind Rappaport.

"Well, the victim's mother, Beverly Jenkins, cared," he said, pointing in her direction. "So did his brother, Tom Jenkins. And, importantly, so did Bellevue Police Detective Casey Emory."

He turned his shoulders back to the jurors. "And after you hear all the evidence in this case, you'll care too."

He paused again and laid a thoughtful hand across his lips. He nodded, then lowered his hand again. "Let me tell you a little about Gerald Jenkins. Jerry."

Brunelle dropped his shoulders slightly, and opened his hands. Disarming gestures. "He wasn't actually the lowest," Brunelle admitted. "The lowest are pretty low. A mentally ill drug addict dying in some back alley and shouting at the police officers and social workers who are trying to help him." A little guilt could be a good thing for a jury. Guilt made people want to do things. Convicting a murderer was doing something. "No, Jerry was above that, but it was maybe an even worse place to be. He wasn't at the bottom. He was invisible. Not poor enough, not disabled enough, not old enough, not mentally ill enough, to get the sympathy and services he might need to make it through this life. He was an able-bodied man in the middle of his life. He was expected to figure it out himself. And if he didn't, well, the rest of us didn't want to hear about it."

Yeah, a little more guilt. It was like the seasoning on the story. If the jurors didn't feel sorry for the victim, they wouldn't care that he was gone. And if they didn't care that he was gone, they might not convict the person who did it. There was no doubt the case would be a million times easier for Brunelle if the person shot to death in that black Audi sedan had been a seven-year-old girl, preferably in pigtails and a pink dress. So, rather than ignore one of the weaknesses in his case—the possibility the jury wouldn't care about the death of some nameless failure—he'd hit them in the face with it.

"Jerry was left to scratch out his existence the best he could," Brunelle continued. "He fought drug addiction and his own bad choices, it eventually becoming impossible to untangle which caused which. And he lived just under the radar in the wealth and privilege that blankets Bellevue and the Eastside."

Another pause. They were like chapter breaks in the story he was telling them. A chance for the jurors to consider what he'd just said before having to listen to what would come next.

"But Jerry wasn't truly invisible," Brunelle went on. "Not to everyone. Oh sure, he was invisible to the good people of the world, like you and me. The people who work in Bellevue's shiny glass office towers. The people who drive to Bellevue Square to shop at the high-end stores. The people visiting the latest organic grocery store or trendy sushi bar. But he wasn't invisible to everyone. In fact, to two groups, he was very visible. His family. And the police."

That was probably a little shocking to at least some of the jurors. Most or all of them had probably only encountered a police officer when they got stopped for speeding that one time. Or maybe those two or three times. But the idea of being well-known by the police, that was foreign. And the idea that the police might have an affinity for you, even as they keep arresting you? That would need to be explained.

"In fact," Brunelle explained, "for better or worse—for better *and* worse—Jerry got to know the local police pretty well. And they got to know him. He was a sort of career misdemeanor criminal. You'll hear from the officers, it was almost like a friendship. Some days, Jerry needed a lift to the shelter. Some days he needed to get checked into drug rehab—*again*. And some days he needed to be arrested. It was a same day, different crime sort of thing. It was almost predictable.

"Until something totally unpredictable happened. Something different. Something terrible. Until the night they didn't arrest him for yet another petty crime. Until the night when they found him dead in a car in an underground garage, two gunshots to the head, and instead of closing the case with an arrest for trespassing, they opened an investigation for murder. Until they set out to figure out what happened to good old Jerry Jenkins."

Brunelle took another moment to let all that sink in. He wanted the jurors to picture the scene. Feel the cool underground air. Hear the echo of the gunshots off the bare concrete. Smell the blood on the ground. Then he continued.

"And here's what happened."

Opening statement was about telling a story. It wasn't just

the first time a lawyer gets to tell the jury what happened, it was the only chance to do it in a normal, chronological, understandable format. Questions and answers from dozens of witnesses put the facts out there, but they didn't make sense without the setup. And even the setup had a setup. All the talk about good old Jerry Jenkins was the setup to make them care about what he was about to say. And believe it.

"Jerry was sitting in his car. A black Audi A4. He hadn't transferred the title yet, but the police will tell you, he'd just bought it used from a friend who owed him a favor. It was a nice car. Probably the nicest one he'd ever owned. And it would be the last.

"He was parked underneath the latest of the glass-and-steel office towers that have sprung up in downtown Bellevue over the last decade or so. The mom-and-pop stores and non-chain restaurants that used to line Bellevue Way are gone now, replaced by high-rises boasting luxury penthouses at the top, executive offices in the middle, and high-end retail shops on the ground floor. And underneath, parking for all the residents and workers and shoppers coming to that one small block in downtown Bellevue every day.

"The parking garage goes down five floors. It also closes at ten p.m., at least the part not gated off for residents. All the workers and shoppers and whoever else are supposed to leave by ten. And most of them do.

"But Jerry didn't."

No crime in that. Well, trespassing, maybe, but not worth mentioning again. They'd crossed over into the murder narrative. He continued the story.

"He was parked on the fourth level down, over in the corner. Out of sight, mostly. The perfect place to hope the night security guards figured you were just a parked car and leave you alone so you can sleep someplace sort of warm that night."

That was the innocent reason for being there. But there were others.

"It was also the perfect place for a crime. Maybe a drug deal, too far from the security cameras to make out the details of the exchange. Maybe drug usage, shooting up in the car away from prying eyes. Or maybe murder.

"Definitely murder.

"Because that's where Jerry Jenkins was parked, sitting in the driver's seat of his new car, when the defendant, Neil Rappaport, walked up from behind and fired two shots into Jerry Jenkins' head."

He was definitely going to let that sink in. That was his whole theory of the case. Everything else was to support that one allegation.

"Jerry never had a chance. He never saw it coming.

"How do we know? We have surveillance video. Now, the camera was too far away to be able to make out details like someone exchanging money for a baggie of drugs. But it wasn't too far away to watch the shooter walk up behind Jerry's car. And it wasn't too far to see the two flashes of the two gunshots that ended Jerry Jenkins's life."

Brunelle took a moment to return to his initial spot, centered before the jury. He raised thoughtful fingers to his lips. "There's no question the video captures the murder of Jerry Jenkins. That's how he died, and that's where he died. And there's a second video, shot from a different angle, of the shooter stepping off the elevator just before murdering Jerry. There's no doubt it captures the murderer. It shows the man who murdered Jerry Jenkins."

He pointed to the defense table. "And that man was Neil Rappaport."

Dramatic. That was important too. Jurors wanted a little drama, at least a little from the safety of their jury box.

"You'll see the video for yourselves," Brunelle promised them. "And you'll see Neil Rappaport's face on that video. The police also recovered a fingerprint from inside the elevator that night, and you'll see that fingerprint belongs to Neil Rappaport. He was the shooter," Brunelle repeated. "He was Jerry Jenkins's murderer."

Brunelle paused again. He couldn't leave it at that. Not quite. The jurors would want all the standard questions answered: who, what, when, where, and why. When and where were formalities. How had just been explained, two gunshots to the head. And Brunelle had just promised them the who was Neil Rappaport. That just left the why.

"But why?" Brunelle asked the question for them. "Well, let's take a moment and admit there can never really be a why for murder. There's never really an excuse. And most of us would never do something like this, no matter how angry we were. So don't expect a 'why' that you can relate with. Unless you could kill a stranger in a parking lot in the middle of the night."

Good. Downplay the 'why.' Make it seem less important. And make his stretch of an explanation seem less far-fetched.

"Well, let me tell you a little about Neil Rappaport," Brunelle continued. "When he was in college, he founded a small computer software company with a friend. Over the years, they tried lots of different products until they hit on a perfect app for these new things called 'smartphones.' Overnight, he became as wealthy as anyone could ever want. All for selling some silly gadget for a few bucks per purchase.

"He got the house on the lake, the car collection, the trips around the world. But apparently it wasn't enough."

Guilt was a great motivator. So was class envy.

"He lived like he was better than everyone else," Brunelle asserted. "Eventually, he felt like he was better than everyone else. And after that, he wanted to prove it.

"There's no other reason," Brunelle admitted. "He didn't know Jerry Jenkins. He didn't care about Jerry Jenkins. When the police went to his home and arrested him for the murder of Jerry Jenkins, he didn't say he was sorry, he didn't pretend he hadn't done it. He just said, 'I don't know who that is.' As if it mattered whether he, the great and powerful Neil Rappaport, knew the identity of the man whose life he had randomly snuffed out."

The jury finally knew what happened. And they sort of knew why—maybe. Time to wrap it up.

"But no one is above the law," Brunelle said. "Not you, not me, and not Neil Rappaport. So at the end of this trial, after you've heard all of the evidence, I will stand up again and ask you to return a verdict of guilty to the crime of Murder in the First Degree.

"Thank you."

Brunelle sat down again, and got a 'good job' pat on the shoulder from Carlisle. But they both knew it wasn't as simple as that. Brunelle looked over to see if old man Voegel would stand up to deliver the defense opening. But no such luck.

Khachaturian was already standing, and so Judge Nguyen said, "Now, ladies and gentlemen, please give your attention to Mr. Khachaturian, who will deliver the opening statement on behalf of the defendant."

CHAPTER 25

Khachaturian took a slightly different position in front of the jury—a half step closer—and held a different posture. Brunelle had stood up as straight as possible, model posture. Khachaturian was shorter, rounder, and stood with a slight slouch. But it was an earnest slouch. A genuine, normal posture. Like he was your friend from work, about to tell you about his weekend.

"Mr. Brunelle just said a lot of things," he started. "A lot of words. A lot of promises. A lot of facts. And a lot of promises. He told you who died. He told you where he died. He told you how he died. But you know what you didn't hear? Not really, anyway? *Why* he died. And more specifically, why my client, Neil Rappaport, would ever have done something so heinous, so senseless, so unforgivable as murdering Gerald Jenkins in cold blood."

Khachaturian didn't just turn and point at Rappaport. He walked over and stood behind him, hands on his shoulders. The jurors had no choice but to look at him.

"Why in the world would a man like Neil Rappaport kill anyone, let alone someone he'd never met?" Khachaturian asked. "The answer is, of course, that he wouldn't. And he didn't."

He clapped his client on the shoulders and returned to his spot in front of the jurors.

"Now, I expect at the end of the trial," Khachaturian continued, "Mr. Brunelle will stand up and tell you he doesn't actually have to prove why someone murdered someone else. And he's correct. Sort of. To a degree. But not completely. Why someone murders someone else is not an element of the crime. First Degree Murder requires a premeditated, intentional killing of another person, without lawful authority. The law doesn't require any particular reason. But..."

He knew how to use pauses as well as Brunelle. He held a finger in the air, as if it were holding that 'but' aloft until he was ready to finish his sentence.

"But," he repeated, "*you* can require it. You can, and should, expect that the prosecution will explain to you not only what happened, but why. Because—and ladies and gentlemen, this is very, important..."

And sometimes you throw out all the little tricks like pauses and hand gestures and pats on the shoulder, and just tell them to listen.

"Because if it doesn't make any sense that Neil Rappaport would have killed Gerald Jenkins, well, then, maybe he didn't."

To that point, all of Khachaturian's opening statement had really been more closing argument. And opening statements weren't supposed to be argumentative—that is, they were supposed to discuss the facts that were expected to be proved, not how those facts might or might not prove the charges. So, Brunelle could have objected as argumentative, and the objection likely would have been sustained. But the jury would also have known that Khachaturian was making valid points, and hurting the prosecution case, and Brunelle didn't want that. Better to play it off, not look directly at

Khachaturian, and pretend to be discussing strategy confidently with his co-counsel. Who, Brunelle could tell, was dying to make that very objection and shut Khachaturian up.

"You're going to hear from a lot of witnesses, I imagine," Khachaturian continued. "At least one of those will be a police detective. Pay attention when my turn comes to ask the detective questions. She'll tell you, the first thing they usually do when trying to solve a murder, is identify suspects who might have wanted to harm the victim. Someone who had a motive. A reason. A why.

"But there's no motive here," Khachaturian said. "No reason. No why.

"Because the evidence will show you, Neil didn't kill anyone. Not Gerald Jenkins, not anyone. Pay attention to the evidence the prosecution puts on. But," another finger in the air to hold that 'but' aloft, "also pay attention to what evidence they don't present."

Khachaturian could point too. He turned and pointed at Brunelle and Carlisle.

"Not only will no witness be able to tell you why Neil would have murdered Mr. Jenkins. Not one witness will identify the man on the surveillance video is Neil. And not one witness will say the fingerprint from the elevator matches Neil's fingerprint.

"In fact, ladies and gentlemen, none of the witnesses will give you enough evidence to conclude anything other than Neil Rappaport is not guilty of the murder of Gerald Jenkins.

"Thank you."

Khachaturian returned to a hearty handshake from his client and whispered compliments from his co-counsel. The battle was joined.

Judge Nguyen looked at the prosecution table. "Call your first witness."

CHAPTER 26

Carlisle stood up. "The State calls Mike Brown to the stand."

Not 'Michael,' just 'Mike.' The security guard who'd found the body. Somehow, 'Mike' worked better. Carlisle had an ear for that sort of thing.

She was doing the first witness because Brunelle had done the opening. It wouldn't be a perfect one-for-one, popping up each after the other like two whack-a-moles, but some divisions would be intentional. It was important for the jury to hear from both of them as soon as possible in the trial. It was also important to divide the heavy lifting; Brunelle had done opening, so Carlisle would do the closing argument. The jury needed to see them as a team, both invested in the prosecution. So, at least two people in the courtroom thought Rappaport was guilty.

Mike Brown entered the courtroom and was sworn in by the judge. Once he'd taken his seat on the witness stand, Carlisle began.

"Please state your name and occupation," she instructed.

"Mike Brown," the witness answered. He was maybe twenty years old, with baby fat still on his face and in need of a haircut. "I'm a security officer with Lincoln Properties Investment

Company."

"How long have you been a security guard with Lincoln Properties?"

"Almost a year," was the answer.

"Have your duties ever included monitoring the parking garages after hours?"

Brown nodded. "That's all my duties have ever included. I work graveyards, and that's the main thing to do on graveyards. I'll be eligible for a transfer after I finish my probation year."

"Okay," Carlisle answered, repeating a common verbal tick on direct-exam. "Do you ever encounter cars parked in the garages after hours?"

Another nod. "Yeah, it's pretty common, actually."

"And what kinds of activities are usually associated with these vehicles?"

Brown's face scrunched up a bit. "Huh?"

Carlisle smiled slightly at herself, and rephrased the overly lawyerly question. "What are people doing in the cars?"

"Oh," Brown replied. "Uh, lots of different things. I mean, a lot of them are just empty. Like maybe somebody went to one of the nightclubs, but then got drunk and took a cab home. If that happens, we don't ticket them or anything. We'd rather have them do that, you know?"

"Sure," Carlisle agreed. "That makes sense. What about the cars where there are still people in them? What are they usually doing?"

"Uh, a lot of them are sleeping," Brown answered. "Especially in the winter. It stays pretty warm down there, compared to up on a cold, rainy street."

"Okay, sleeping," Carlisle repeated. "Anything else?"

Brown smiled a little awkwardly. "Well, one thing that

happens kinda more than you might think is people having sex."

Brunelle had to smile at that. He was pretty sure Carlisle wasn't expecting that answer. The jurors seemed to think it was funny too.

"Wow," Carlisle responded. "I wouldn't have thought that, but okay. Anything else? Drug use maybe?"

It was a leading question, but he needed to be led a bit.

"Oh, right," Brown confirmed. "That happens a lot too. I mean, I think so. I find people who are passed out and won't wake up. So we call the fire department and they take the person to the hospital."

"Have you ever seen a drug deal?"

Brown shook his head. "No, but then again, I wear a uniform that has a badge on the front and says 'Security' in big huge letters on my back. If that's going on, they probably see me coming before I see them."

Carlisle didn't offer her 'okay' back. She was about to switch gears slightly.

"What about murder?" she asked. "Has that ever happened?"

Brown frowned, suddenly pulled back from unconscious druggies and frisky lovers. "Yeah. Once."

Carlisle stepped away from the witness then and fetched a photo from where the exhibits had been laid out on the counter in front of the bailiff. She returned and handed it to Brown.

"Do you recognize what's depicted in that photo?" she asked.

Brown took a moment, then nodded. "Yeah. That's where I found the guy who'd been killed."

"Is that an accurate depiction of what the scene looked like that night when you found the guy who'd been killed?"

Brown took a moment. "Yeah. There's some crime scene tape in the background that wasn't there until the cops showed up, but yeah, that's definitely the dude that got shot."

'*The dude that got shot.*' Brunelle wrote the phrase on his notepad. He would remind Carlisle not to refer to Jerry Jenkins as that during her closing.

Carlisle moved to admit the photograph and show it to the jury. Khachaturian didn't object. She put the photo on the projector and the screen on the far wall filled with the image of a black Audi, driver's door open, body slumped over the wheel, blood everywhere. She'd leave it up on the wall for the remainder of her examination.

"Tell us," she instructed her witness, "how you came to find Jerry Jenkins murdered in his car."

Brown took a moment to gather his thoughts, then began. "I was doing my regular rounds. I start at the top and take the stairs down one flight at a time. It's easier than starting at the bottom and climbing the stairs. And I have to check all the stairwells because homeless people try to sleep there sometimes."

"Okay," Carlisle encouraged him to continue.

"So, I had just finished the second floor and was about to go down to the third floor when I heard two loud bangs."

"Like gunshots?" Carlisle suggested.

"Well, yeah. I know that now," Brown answered. "But back then, I didn't think they were gunshots. I mean, that's what it sounded like, but come on, it's Bellevue. That stuff doesn't happen in Bellevue. I figured it was somebody breaking something. That does happen in Bellevue."

"Okay," Carlisle gave him that. "Then what happened?"

"So, I went down to three and looked around really quick from the stairwell. I didn't see anything, so I went down to four. I figured I could go back to three once I figured out what the noise was. But if somebody was breaking something, I needed to take care of that right away, see if I could stop them."

"And what did you see when you got to four?"

Brown pointed up at the screen. "I saw that. I mean from a distance. At first, I thought maybe the person in there had been the one making the noise. So I walked up and, well, that's when I realized what I heard was probably gunshots."

"Did you go all the way up to the driver's door?" Carlisle asked.

"Yeah, pretty much," Brown answered. "You couldn't really see anything 'til you were right up on it. I was trying to see inside as I walked up. Figured I might see someone passed out, or having sex, or whatever."

"But it wasn't anything like that, was it?"

Brown looked up at the photo again. "No, ma'am."

"So what did you do?"

"I called 911."

"Did you try to help him?" Carlisle asked.

"No," Brown answered.

"Why not?"

Brown frowned. "I didn't think I was going to be able to help him. I mean it was pretty obvious he'd been shot in the head. There was blood all in his hair and on his face and all over the windshield. There wasn't really anything I could do, you know?"

"Okay. Did the police respond?" Carlisle asked.

"Yeah, and the fire department," Brown answered.

"Did you stay near the car from the time you called 911 until police and fire arrived?"

"Yes, ma'am."

"And did anyone approach the car during that time?"

"No, ma'am."

Carlisle nodded. One last question. "You said you took the stairs that night. Would you have seen someone who used the elevators?"

Brown thought for a moment. "Only if they were getting on or off right when I walked by doing my rounds. But otherwise, no. People don't sleep in the elevators, so I don't check them. I just check the stairs."

"Thank you, Mr. Brown," Carlisle said. Then, to the judge, "No further questions."

She sat down and Khachaturian stood up. Brunelle wondered what kind of cross-examination he'd do. So far, he'd been impressive. The motions had been effective and his opening was solid. But a lot of defense attorneys lost steam during cross-exam. The best cross was focused, laser-like, on whatever one or two issues the defense was hanging its hat on. More common, though, was the 'once more from the top' method of cross, where the defense attorney took the witness through everything a second time. Brunelle enjoyed that sort of cross because it not only allowed the witness to tell his or her story a second time, but it might bring out details he'd forgotten to elicit. But unfortunately, Khachaturian seemed intent on justifying that 'Top Litigator' award.

"I have just a few questions, Mr. Brown." The comment was also intended to let the jury know if he sat down quickly, it was by design, not because the witness had somehow bested him. "You got a look at the man's face, correct? You said it was covered in blood, I believe?"

"Yeah," Brown answered. "I didn't look real close, but I did look."

"And you had met Jerry Jenkins before, right?" Khachaturian asked. "In fact, he's previously been trespassed from all Lincoln properties for drug use, so you would have been on the lookout for him."

"There's a lot of people who get trespassed from stuff like that," Brown agreed. "But yeah, we look out for people we know aren't supposed to be there."

"And Jerry Jenkins was one of those people, wasn't he?"

Brown nodded. "Yeah."

"So, you knew Jerry Jenkins, and you would have been on the lookout for him," Khachaturian repeated, "but you didn't recognize him when you saw him in the car, did you?"

Brown shook his head. "No, sir. There was too much blood. And, well, I mean... I think part of his face was missing, honestly. It was pretty gross." He looked around at the judge, and Carlisle, and the gallery that probably held family members. "Sorry."

"No need to apologize," Khachaturian responded. "You're supposed to tell the truth." He nodded toward the photo which he hadn't taken down when he started his exam. Obviously a conscious decision, not an oversight. "That is a very disturbing scene."

Then back to his questions. Or, more accurately, the last question. "So you would agree with me then, that, depending on the circumstances, it can be difficult to positively identify someone from just a short view of them, even if you already know them?"

Brown thought for a moment. He shrugged. "I didn't recognize him. That's all I can say."

But it didn't matter. The jury heard the question, and that was the point, Brunelle knew.

"No further questions," Khachaturian said.

Carlisle elected not to redirect. They had their first witness under their belt. Only a few dozen more to go.

CHAPTER 27

The rest of that first day had been similar first responders. Setting the scene—the 'gross' scene—for the jury to sleep on before returning the next morning to hear from Jerry's family. They could have started with the family, and Brunelle had done that before, but every case was different. And so was every family. He didn't want to start with Beverly and Tom, not least because they didn't like him. That wasn't the first thing he wanted telegraphed to the jurors. As it was, they got to feel shock at the brutality of the murder scene. Next they could feel sympathy for the victim. Shock plus sympathy would make them want to hold someone responsible. And Brunelle had just the person in mind.

Brunelle and Carlisle stayed a little late, each confirming the other was ready for the next day, but eventually hunger forced the decision between staying there all night or going home. They were as ready as they could be. They went home.

Brunelle nuked two frozen dinners and ate straight from the trays. No dishes. One thing he didn't want during trial was extra chores. And one thing he did want was a Manhattan—but, when he went to mix himself one to end his evening, he realized he was out of vermouth.

"Damn."

So the questions were, did he want a Manhattan that much more than straight bourbon, and if so, was he really going to walk all the way to the store to get it?

He looked out the window. It was a nice night. And a walk might do him good. Maybe he'd sleep better after some fresh air. And a Manhattan. He grabbed his wallet and keys and headed out into the evening.

It was a little chilly, but it actually felt good after the stuffy warmth of his condo. The neighborhood was a mix of small-office and boutique retail, a little too far from downtown to serve anyone except the residents, like Brunelle, who couldn't afford the condos closer in. His destination stood six blocks north, with absolutely nothing else open between it and Brunelle's condo building, except the bar directly across the street. But he wanted to make his own drink and sip it as he got ready for bed, not pay for a full cocktail and drink it sitting on a barstool late on a weeknight.

The store in question was sort of half grocery store, half convenience store, with semi-fresh fruit, a wall of candy bars, and a healthy selection of booze for the urban alcohol- and drug-addicted clientele it served. Brunelle grabbed the smaller bottle of sweet vermouth and a bag of chips then got in line behind a man trying to buy a 20-ounce malt liquor with coins. He didn't quite have enough. Brunelle considered paying the difference, but he wasn't sure if that was a nice thing to do or not. Before he could decide, the clerk told the man it was good enough, and scooped the balance out of the tip jar.

"Just these?" the clerk asked as Brunelle set his items on the counter.

"Yep," he confirmed, and a card swipe and brown bag later,

Brunelle was making his way six blocks south to a smooth drink and a warm bed.

It was somehow even quieter out than on his way there. There was no one else out.

Except that guy standing in the shadow next to the approaching alleyway. Brunelle squinted into the shadow. Make that two guys.

Brunelle frowned. He also crossed the street. He could cross back in front of the bar, which suddenly seemed very far away.

He kept his eye on the two figures in the shadows. He couldn't tell if they were watching him too, but they weren't making any effort to follow him to the other side of the street. That was good.

Until Matthias the Giant stepped out from the alleyway on Brunelle's side of the street.

"Hello again," he said as Brunelle stopped up short.

Fuck. He thought. But he didn't say it. He didn't say 'Hello' either.

"Matthias, right?" Brunelle started. Man, he really was a lot bigger than Brunelle. And younger. And those two guys were crossing the street after all. "Look, I don't want any trouble."

Matthias frowned. "You know my name?"

Brunelle hoped the lack of anonymity might discourage what was obviously a plan to scare and/or assault him. "Yeah. Vickie mentioned you."

A flash of emotions crossed Matthias's face, but it was hard to tell exactly what in the half-light. Also, Brunelle didn't really care, except inasmuch as it might help him talk his way out of the situation. Although he wasn't really sure about how to do that right then, what with the blood rushing in his ears.

"I told you to stay away from her," Matthias said.

"Yes, you did," Brunelle replied. "And by a strange coincidence, we called it off a few weeks ago. I haven't seen her since then. So, there you go. Problem solved."

Matthias narrowed his eyes at Brunelle. "I don't believe you. That's not what Vickie said."

Brunelle shrugged. "Yeah, I don't really know what to say to that. But I haven't talked to Vickie for weeks. So, you know, knock yourself out."

Matthias thought for a moment, then he smiled. "Or," he said just before he punched Brunelle in the mouth, "I could knock you out."

Brunelle fell backward onto the sidewalk. Luckily, he hit ass-first, before his shoulders and finally his head hit. It hurt, but he was grateful not to have landed head first. He'd seen more than one manslaughter case where a single punch knocked out the victim, who didn't try to break their fall, literally cracked their skull on the pavement, then died from the resultant brain bleed. The only thing on Brunelle that was bleeding was his mouth. But that was more than enough.

The vermouth had gone flying, breaking on impact. Brunelle pushed himself back to his feet. He stood for a moment, still crouching, and wiped the blood from his mouth with the back of his hand.

"You know what, Matthias?" he said. "Maybe I will look up good ol' Vickie again. Shit, maybe I'll even drop by her place tonight. And fuck the shit out of her like I've already done a bunch of times."

Matthias roared and took another swing, but Brunelle was ready for it. Hell, he'd provoked it. He grabbed Matthias's arm and pulled, throwing him off balance and into the wall of the building they were next to. When he turned back, Brunelle punched him in the face, a glancing blow off his cheek. But that was as good as Brunelle was going to get in. The other two tackled him to the ground. He covered up as punches rained down on his head. But they stopped sooner than he feared. He'd read those autopsy reports too.

Matthias knelt on his chest and grabbed his shirt. "You stay away from her. You don't deserve her."

Brunelle managed a smile through his swelling lips. "You're not the first person to tell me that."

"You don't know her," Matthias went on. You don't care about her. You just want her money."

Brunelle was bleeding, embarrassed, angry, scared, and a half dozen other emotions. But he was still a lawyer. And lawyers hate unsupportable assertions.

"Her money?" he laughed. "She doesn't have any money, dumb ass. Rappaport divorced her."

"She gets half his company then," Matthias asserted.

"No, he kept his share of the company. She only gets alimony. And she won't even get that after Rappaport goes to prison. You think he can send her ten grand a month when he's making ten cents an hour?"

Matthias didn't say anything. Brunelle could read the emotion on his face then. He spat blood up at him. "You idiot. You thought you were going to get rich? Joke's on you. No one's getting rich, except maybe Paul Cross. Maybe you should date him."

Matthias punched Brunelle one more time in the side of his face. "Fuck you." Then, as almost an effort to salvage the justification for the attack, "Stay away from her anyway."

Then he pushed off Brunelle, knocking the wind out of him, and stormed off with his henchmen. Brunelle rolled onto his side and tried to catch his breath. He knew not to take too long, in case the three of them decided to return and take out further frustration on him. He forced himself into a sitting position and looked over at the brown bag a few feet away, soaked through from the spilled vermouth.

"I should've known drinking was bad for my health."

CHAPTER 28

Brunelle did his best to clean up, but even his second best dark suit, another bright white shirt, and a gorgeous gold necktie couldn't cover up the cuts and bruises on his face.

Carlisle's eyes flew wide when she saw him. "Wow. I take it back. You looked great yesterday." Then, "What the hell happened to you?"

"I fell down the stairs," he quipped. "Into a door. It was my fault."

Nothing like a little dark domestic violence humor to deflect a question.

"Seriously," Carlisle said. "Are you okay?"

Brunelle nodded. "Yeah, I'm fine. You should see the other guy."

"Oh yeah?" Carlisle raised an expectant eyebrow.

But Brunelle shook his head. "No, not really. I only got one good shot in, and it wasn't even that good a shot. There were three of them."

"Sure there were," Carlisle grinned. "Probably five or six. And one of them was Batman."

"I wish one of them had been Batman," Brunelle said. "I'm pretty sure I was the victim. He would have avenged me."

Carlisle shook her head. "No, the other guys do the avenging. He's a Justice League guy."

Brunelle closed his eyes and shook his head. He would have pinched the bridge of his nose, but it was swollen and tender. "Whatever. Anyway, it's over and I'm ready for trial. Let's just drop it."

Carlisle was willing to drop it, even if only because she'd gotten her jabs in—so to speak. But everyone else in the courtroom was most definitely still looking at him and whispering to each other. Then the judge came out.

"Are the parties rea--?" she started to ask, until she saw Brunelle's battered face. "Mr. Brunelle, what happened to you?"

Brunelle stood up to address the court. "It's a long story, Your Honor." His speech was slurred slightly by the swelling in and around his mouth. "I'd rather not delay the proceedings with it. We're ready to proceed."

Judge Nguyen frowned. "I'm not sure we are," she said. "You look terrible. Have you seen a doctor?"

Brunelle shook his head. "I'm fine, Your Honor. I promise. We're ready. Ms. Carlisle can do the majority of the witnesses today."

He hadn't told Carlisle that yet, but he knew she could, and would, handle it.

"I'll look a lot better tomorrow," he added.

Judge Nguyen nodded. "Tomorrow it is, then. I'm not going to rush this trial. And I'm not going to have one of my lawyers suddenly appear to have been assaulted. Who knows what the jurors might think of that? Imaginations could run wild. For all we know, they might assume the defendant planned the attack as retribution for the prosecution. and none of us will address it sufficiently to identify, let alone stop, that sort of speculation."

Brunelle's shoulders dropped. He didn't want to be the reason for any delays. Especially not for getting beat up. But he wasn't going to protest. Further protest would require further explanation, and further explanation would probably require mentioning Vickie's name. That could send the entire prosecution into a tailspin.

"Yes, Your Honor," he said. "Thank you, Your Honor."

Judge Nguyen instructed her bailiff to tell the jurors that the court had a sudden and unexpected scheduling conflict and they would start first thing the next morning. Brunelle turned around to apologize to Beverly and Tom, but they were already motoring toward the exit. He turned back to Carlisle, who had crossed arms and was both smiling and shaking her head.

"It's always about you, isn't it, Dave?" she laughed.

But Brunelle frowned. "That's just it. I don't think it really had anything to do with me."

CHAPTER 29

The next day, the swelling was down considerably, aided by an evening of aggressive icing, and Carlisle gave him some makeup to cover the redness of the cuts on his mouth and under his eye. From a distance, with his hand blocking most of his face, Brunelle was mostly presentable.

So they presented to the jury. Nguyen called them out and Carlisle stood to announce their next witness. She was still going to do the day's examinations.

"The State calls Beverly Jenkins," she declared.

Mrs. Jenkins rolled slowly to the front of the courtroom, where the judge swore her in even as the bailiff removed the chair from the witness stand. Beverly motored up the ramp and after a few stops and starts, straightened herself out to face Carlisle for the questioning.

Beverly's job was simple. She hadn't been out to the murder scene. She hadn't witnessed the murder. She really didn't know anything about what happened. But the prosecution was allowed to introduce one photograph of the murder victim while he or she was still alive. To remind the jury that the victim was once a living, breathing person—until Rappaport murdered him. Those photos were called, appropriately enough, the 'in-life photos' and there was no better person to introduce one of those through than the victim's mother. Especially since, otherwise, Beverly Jenkins didn't have anything relevant to say. But you always want the mother on the stand. Always.

Carlisle had her identify herself by name and as Gerald Jenkins's mother. Then she had her identify the photo as one that she had found and provided to the prosecution. It was from a family gathering of some sort, probably Thanksgiving judging by the sweaters and leaves on the ground. She confirmed that was her sweet baby boy, even as a grown adult, and even with all of his problems.

Carlisle didn't ask about those problems. She didn't ask about drug use, or criminal activity. That could come out through Emory. A mother shouldn't have to talk about that sort of thing. Especially not at the trial for her child's murder.

The photo was admitted, the mother was introduced, and Carlisle was done. She announced, "No further questions" and all eyes turned to Khachaturian, who, despite his ever-present co-counsel, seemed to be trying the case alone after all.

Brunelle wondered if he might step into the trap and expose himself to the jury as the heartless shark Brunelle wanted them to think he was. But no such luck. He stood just long enough to say, "No questions."

You don't cross-examine the mom.

But you might cross-examine the brother.

Tom Jenkins was next. He could identify Jerry from the same family photo. But more importantly, he'd been the one who'd had to identify his brother at the morgue. And it was important for the jury to know the victim hadn't just been alive, he'd been loved.

When Carlisle finished with him, Khachaturian stood again, and stepped out from behind the counsel table.

"I'm sorry for your loss," he started, "but I do need to ask you a few questions about your brother."

The apology wasn't for Tom; it was for the jury. Khachaturian didn't give a crap about what Tom Jenkins thought of him, but he wanted the jury to think he was a nice guy. Some of that might rub off on his client.

Tom just nodded in response.

"Were you aware," Khachaturian asked delicately, "of any criminal activity involving your brother?"

Tom frowned. "You mean like getting murdered by your client?"

Khachaturian winced. "I suppose the murder would technically meet the parameters of my question," he said. "But no, I mean criminal activity by your brother? Drug use, perhaps? Or even drug dealing?"

Brunelle knew the dealing part was important. Junkies using drugs in the garage would just pass out. It was the dealers who risked getting ripped off by a buyer who decided to take the drugs and keep his money. A drug rip. And a drug rip gone bad is probably what the police would have thought happened if it hadn't been for that video.

Tom crossed his arms. "No."

"No to drug dealing?" Khachaturian tried to clarify. "Or no to all of it?"

"All of it," Tom practically growled. "Jerry was a good guy. He'd had a rough life, but he didn't deserve what happened to him, if that's what you're suggesting."

Khachaturian shook his head. "Oh, no. I'm not suggesting that at all. I just thought, as his brother, you might have more insight into your brother's activities and any problems he might have been having."

"No problems," Tom insisted. "He'd had problems in the past. But not any more. He was clean and he was doing great. Just great. And then Neil Rappaport murdered him."

Khachaturian sighed a little. Brunelle knew he was being forced to ask a question outside of his prepared line of questioning. "You didn't actually see my client murder your brother, right?"

"Right," Tom confirmed. "But I know it. I've seen the evidence and I know he did it."

Brunelle looked up slightly, trying not to betray his still-healing wounds. He hadn't shared the evidence with Tom Jenkins, or any other witness for that matter. He knew not to do that. A lesser defense attorney might have seized on that and turned to accuse Brunelle of coaching or even tampering with a witness. But Khachaturian returned to his main point, which was actually just a trap. "So, your testimony is that your brother was off drugs and not involved in any criminal activity at all at the time of his death?"

"His murder," Tom corrected him. "And yes."

Khachaturian nodded. "Thank you, no further questions."

Carlisle looked to Brunelle. They both knew Tom had just lied to the jury—committed perjury, if you wanted to get technical—and if the jury didn't already also know it, they would after Emory testified. Heck, even Mike Brown had already said he was trespassing. But there was no way to undo that damage without risking Tom doubling, or even tripling down. Blood was thicker than truth.

Brunelle shook his head slightly. Carlisle nodded hers in reply, and stood up. "No redirect, Your Honor. This witness can be excused." Tom stalked out of the courtroom, staring down both Khachaturian and Rappaport as he went. Brunelle was just glad he wasn't staring down him and Carlisle.

The last witness to introduce Gerald Jenkins to the jury wasn't family. It was the medical examiner. Dr. Emil Kaladi. Beverly and Tom had told the jurors about how Jerry had lived. Dr. Kaladi would tell them how he died.

CHAPTER 30

Khachaturian kept to the short and sweet cross-examinations. Carlisle took nearly an hour to guide Kaladi through the autopsy. He explained about gunshot wounds, how to tell the difference between an entrance and an exit wound (entrance wounds are like hole punches, exit wounds are tears), and why a bullet can lose enough velocity going through one side of the skull that it doesn't have enough power left to get through the other side, resulting in it ricocheting repeatedly through the brain.

Like what happened to Jerry Jenkins.

It was worth the time to make the jury suffer through the testimony, and the photographs—oh, the photographs—so the jurors could feel the revulsion of the death, and maybe, just maybe, imagine the pain Jerry Jenkins would have felt as his brain was scrambled by the bullet fired from Neil Rappaport's gun.

But then Khachaturian stood up and cut to the chase. "Doctor, you can tell a person died of gunshot wounds, but you can't tell who fired those shots, can you?"

Dr. Kaladi had no trouble agreeing. "Correct. I can tell you a death is a homicide. But I can't tell you who did it."

"And even less so, why they did it?" Khachaturian followed up.

"Oh, heavens no," Dr. Kaladi agreed. "That's well beyond my abilities. Although…" Kaladi added before Khachaturian could stop him, "in my experience there are really only two reasons why anyone kills anyone else."

Khachaturian had gotten the answer he'd wanted: Kaladi couldn't say why Neil Rappaport would have murdered Jerry Jenkins. He should have sat down again at that point, but Kaladi's last comment was too intriguing to leave it hanging, even if only because the jury wanted to know the answer. And a good trial never disappoints the jury.

He nodded to the doctor. "And what are those?"

Kaladi looked to the jurors to deliver his wisdom. "Love," he said, "or money."

Khachaturian seemed okay with that answer. His client wasn't dating Jerry Jenkins as far as anyone knew, and he didn't need money.

"Thank you, Doctor."

Carlisle didn't do any redirect-exam. The 'love or money' comment was personal opinion, interesting but hardly rebuttable. They were ready to move on. The next big witness would be Det. Emory.

CHAPTER 31

The last part of their case-in-chief was going to be tricky. Normally, if Nguyen hadn't knocked their feet out from under them, they would have finished with the world-renowned Maxwell Hutchinson pointing at the blown-up still from the surveillance video and telling the jury, 'The murderer, ladies and gentleman, is none other than the defendant, Neil Rappaport.'

As it was, if they finished with that scenario, Hutchinson would point at the image, then say nothing, while Brunelle did his best to make a wide-eyed, 'Do you see it?' expression to the jury, his own argument that it was a match prohibited until closings, which could be days later.

They couldn't finish with that. Start strong, end strong. So that meant they would finish with Emory, then O'Rourke, then Hutchinson. But not necessarily in that order.

"The State calls Detective Casey Emory to the stand," Brunelle announced as they entered the final sprint of their case.

The detective entered the courtroom and was sworn in as Brunelle readied himself for the examination. His injuries had mostly healed up, with no more swelling affecting his speech, so he was good to jump back in and be a partner to his partner. Besides, he had liked Emory from the moment he'd met her. He wanted to do her questioning.

"Please state your name for the record," he began, as with pretty much every other witness he'd ever examined.

"Casey Emory," the detective answered.

"How are you employed?"

"I'm a detective with the Bellevue Police Department."

"Are you assigned to any particular division?"

Emory turned and told the jury directly, "I'm assigned to the violent crimes unit."

"Is there a homicide unit?" Brunelle asked.

Emory smiled slightly and shook her head. "No. Bellevue doesn't need a separate homicide division."

Then Brunelle led her through the incident. The initial call out. Her first observations. Her preliminary thoughts. She looked again at the photos admitted earlier through witnesses like Mike Brown, the crime scene technicians, and even the clipboard guy. But Emory wasn't just another officer. She was a detective. The lead detective. It wasn't her job to document the crime; it was her job to solve it.

"Once you secured the scene and were briefed by the other officers," Brunelle asked her, "what were the first steps you took to try to identify the shooter?"

"I contacted Ken Tanner, the head of security for Lincoln Properties to see if the murder might have been captured on video."

"And was it?"

Again, Emory turned to the jurors. "Yes."

Then Brunelle didn't ask her if she'd watched it. Instead, he asked her if she collected the video and put it into evidence.

Emory seemed a bit surprised, but answered the question. "Uh, yes. Mr. Tanner made copies of the relevant surveillance videos and I booked them into the evidence room when I returned to Bellevue P.D. headquarters."

Brunelle nodded. "Did you collect any other evidence from the garage?" Of course, he knew, so he clarified. "Fingerprints or anything like that?"

"I didn't collect the fingerprint myself," Emory explained. "But yes, Dan O'Rourke, one of our fingerprint technicians, successfully recovered a latent fingerprint on the 'close door' button of the elevator."

"What did you do with that recovered fingerprint?"

"When a fingerprint is located," Emory explained, "the technician transfers it to a collection card by applying fingerprint dust to it, then lifting it off with a special type of tape. The tape is then adhered to a fingerprint card and that card was also booked into evidence."

Brunelle nodded and considered for a moment. Then he announced, "No further questions."

Emory looked a little confused, but quickly pivoted to prepare herself for whatever the defense attorney might throw at her.

"You forgot the whole 'I don't know who that is' thing," Carlisle whispered to Brunelle as he returned to his seat next to her.

"No, I didn't," he whispered without looking at her. His gaze was fixed on Khachaturian, approaching the detective to start his cross-examination.

"You're a detective in the violent crimes unit, is that right?" he started.

"Correct," Emory confirmed.

"And in that capacity, you've investigated homicides?"

Khachaturian followed up.

Emory nodded. "Yes, sir. As I said. Bellevue doesn't get a lot of homicides, but I handled this case."

"You also have received training about solving homicides, I take it?"

"Yes," Emory answered. Again, she turned to the jury and listed off the various conferences and courses she'd taken over the years regarding the investigation of homicides and other major violent crimes.

"Would you consider yourself an expert on homicide investigation?" Khachaturian asked.

Brunelle could see Carlisle looked askance at him out of the corner of his eye, but he kept his attention focused on Emory and her questioner.

Emory considered for a moment. "I consider myself a detective," she said. "I investigate violent crimes and I try to do the best job I can."

Khachaturian sighed slightly at the evasion. "All right then. So as a detective, your main job is to solve whatever crime you're investigating, correct?"

Emory thought for a moment, then agreed. "I think that's a fair statement."

"And part of that is trying to figure out why a person might have committed the crime, correct?"

"It can be," Emory knew to answer. "But it doesn't have to be. Sometimes there's no good reason why someone commits a crime."

"No good reason," Khachaturian repeated. "But there's usually some reason, isn't there?"

"I suppose," Emory conceded.

"In fact," Khachaturian pressed, "isn't it standard practice to develop a list of suspects based on who would have had a reason to commit the crime?"

"Standard procedure?" Emory clarified. "Every case is different."

"Fine," Khachaturian huffed. "Homicide cases. Murder cases. When you find a murder victim, don't you try to figure out who might have had a reason to murder the victim?"

"There are a lot of reasons why people commit murder," Emory responded.

Khachaturian smiled, despite the avoidance of his actual question. "Okay," he said. "What are those reasons?"

Emory thought for a moment, then told the jury, "Every case is different of course, but one of the main types of murder is domestic violence. Other common scenarios are robberies gone wrong, gang violence, and young men with too much testosterone and alcohol and not enough sense to back down from a challenge."

Khachaturian smiled again, a little broader, and turned to face the jury as he asked the detective his next series of questions. He probably thought it was dramatic. Brunelle found it overly theatrial and off-putting. He hoped the jurors agreed.

"Was Gerald Jenkins in a dating relationship with my client?

Emory hesitated. "Uh, no," she answered. "Not that I know of."

"Would it make sense for a man of Mr. Rappaport's means to try to rob a man of Mr. Jenkins' means?"

"I wouldn't think so," Emory agreed.

"Is Mr. Rappaport in a street gang?"

"No, sir."

"And do you have any information that either Mr. Rappaport or Mr. Jenkins got into an argument that night at a bar, perhaps over the affections of some young lady?"

"No," Emory replied. "They were both in the parking garage that night."

Khachaturian turned back to her with a sudden jerk of his head. "So you say. But then again, none of the usual reasons for a murder apply to Mr. Rappaport, do they?"

"That's not really what I meant," Emory tried.

But Khachaturian wouldn't have it. "Do they?" he demanded.

Emory grimaced. "No, sir," she admitted.

"No further questions," Khachaturian announced with a flourish of his hand.

Brunelle stood up for just a bit of redirect-exam. "Detective, do you follow the evidence or does the evidence follow you?"

"I follow the evidence," she answered. "I don't come into a case expecting it to be anything other than whatever it is."

"So you don't assume every murder is domestic violence, or a robbery, or two drunk guys in a bar parking lot?"

"Absolutely not, sir."

"Are there ever murders committed that don't fall neatly into one of those scenarios?"

"This one sure didn't," Emory answered.

Brunelle nodded. "Thank you, Detective. No further questions."

Khachaturian didn't conduct any recross, and Emory stepped down from the witness stand. Then, as Carlisle stood up to call the next witness—"The State calls Daniel O'Rourke"—Brunelle slipped out of the courtroom to fetch the fingerprint from the hallway. And grab Emory before she headed back across the lake.

"Don't go anywhere," he told her.

Her expression, which had been a combination of concern

over whether her answers had been good enough and lingering confusion over the subjects discussed and not discussed, warmed up.

"Can you read me now?" he asked.

She narrowed her eyes and appraised him. "I'm not sure. You're all caught up in how you act in front of the jury. But," she smiled, "I trust you."

He smiled back, pulling slightly at one of the still healing cuts in the corner of his mouth. "Good."

Then he ducked back inside to watch Carlisle try to direct examine a fingerprint expert who couldn't tell the jury the fingerprints matched.

It wasn't pretty.

Actually, it wasn't ugly either. It was just anticlimactic.

O'Rourke gave his experience and qualifications. He explained how fingerprints are left on different surfaces. Smooth, hard surfaces—like an elevator button—were best. He confirmed Emory's description of using dust, tape, and a card to lift the print for later analysis. And he explained, in general terms, what kinds of characteristics they compared between the latent and the reference print, and how many of those needed to be the same before they would call it a match.

And then he didn't call it a match.

They blew the prints up on the screen. The one from the elevator button on the left. The one taken from Rappaport at booking on the right. O'Rourke stood up and used a pointer to indicate the eight locations that appeared to be the same on both prints. Then he sat down again. And so did Carlisle.

"No further questions," she had to say. It was like leading a horse to water and not letting him drink.

Their only hope was that Khachaturian might open the door

to the match by challenging O'Rourke's methodology or something. But if Khachaturian had shown one thing, it was that he wasn't stupid. He stayed as far away from that as he could.

"A fingerprint tells us that someone was in a particular place at some point," he said, "but it doesn't tell us when, does it?"

O'Rourke had to agree. "Correct. It was sometime prior to the latent being collected, of course, but I can't tell you how long prior. Not from the print anyway."

"You can't carbon date the fingerprint or anything to determine that it was left at a particular date and time, correct?"

"No, sir. We can't do that. Fingerprints do degrade over time, but there are too many variables to do that. Heat, cold, weather, other persons touching the same area, those would all affect the print in different ways at different times and places."

"So a fingerprint left on, say, an elevator button just means that the person pressed the button sometime in the past, correct?"

"Correct."

"And if no one else pressed the button for, say, I don't know two days or two weeks or two months, that fingerprint would still be there, correct?"

"That is correct sir."

"It doesn't mean the person pressed the button the same night you collected the print, correct?"

"Correct."

Khachaturian offered the witness a smile and a nod. "Thank you. "No further questions."

Carlisle stood up to redirect, still feeling the sting of Khachaturian's cross, but then thought better of it. It wasn't like he was wrong. "No questions, Your Honor."

And O'Rourke was excused. They were almost done.

Brunelle stood up. "The State calls Maxwell Hutchinson."

CHAPTER 32

Again, Hutchinson should have been the dramatic final witness that drove the last nail in Rappaport's coffin—so to speak. But again, he wasn't allowed to be. He could point at the nail, but he had to hand the hammer to Brunelle, and Brunelle had to set the hammer on his table until the end of the trial, then ask the jury to do the pounding.

But Brunelle wasn't going to let the judge ruin his case completely. Hutchinson couldn't spike the ball. But he could set it.

"Please state your name for the record," Brunelle began again.

Then it was occupation, experience, awards, and that story about Dieter from Berlin. It was a good story. The jury seemed to like it anyway.

Then the Gerald Jenkins case. He'd reviewed the video. He'd examined the video. He'd even manipulated the video to make the images even cleaner, even clearer. Khachaturian objected; Nguyen overruled it. Then Brunelle put one of those clean, clear images up on the screen. Right next to Rappaport's driver's license photo.

It wasn't a perfect match. Rappaport hadn't gone to the

DMV with dark clothes and a plan to murder someone. And they hadn't taken his photo in a dark parking garage using a still from video surveillance system. But it was him. Brunelle could see it. He hoped the jury could too.

Still, Khachaturian was right: no witness was going to say it was a match. And without that, the jurors might not either. Undoubtedly, they were expecting a witness, some witness, to say it was a match. The failure of any of them to do so might lead one or more of the jurors to doubt their own eyes and conclude maybe it wasn't a match after all. They needed someone to confirm their own perception. Someone they could trust. Someone they could like.

"No further questions," Brunelle announced and he returned to the prosecution table. He also left the two images of Rappaport up on the screen. This time, though, Khachaturian turned off the projector before proceeding with his cross-examination.

"It sounds like, Mr. Hutchinson," he began, "you've worked on some very interesting cases."

Hutchinson grinned. "I guess I have. Yes."

"And a lot of those cases were murders, weren't they?"

The grin evaporated. "Yes, I'm afraid so," he said, suddenly grim.

"And while every case is different," Khachaturian said, "there are certain patterns that start to emerge if you look at enough cases, wouldn't you agree?"

"I suppose that's probably true," Hutchinson allowed.

"In fact," Khachaturian said, "the medical examiner in this very case previously testified that, in his experience, most murders were committed for love or money. Would you agree with that?"

Hutchinson frowned. "Well, I think it's probably a little more nuanced than that."

"The lead detective in this case," Khachaturian continued, "said, in her experience, most murders were either domestic violence, robberies gone bad, street gangs, or two drunk guys fighting over a girl at a bar. Would you agree with that?"

Hutchinson thought for a moment. "Sounds like basically the same thing," he quipped. "D.V. and the girl at the bar would arguably fall into the 'love' category, and gang turf wars and botched robberies into the 'money' category."

Khachaturian smiled broadly at that. "You're right, Mr. Hutchinson. You have a keen mind for this."

"Thank you," Hutchinson replied. He liked being noticed, and flattered.

"Mr. Hutchinson," Khachaturian went on, "you examined all of the footage from the parking garage that night, didn't you?"

"I did, yes," Hutchinson agreed.

"Not just the parts we've seen in court," Khachaturian clarified, "but every last hour of footage, looking for anything related to this case, correct?"

"That's correct. I always review as much video as I possibly can in every case I consult on."

"Good for you," Khachaturian replied. "Good for you. And in all that video, did you see anything that indicated this murder was related to some sort of romantic relationship between the shooter and the victim?"

Hutchinson considered for a moment. "No, I didn't see anything like that."

"No passionate embraces by the side of the Audi or anything?" Khachaturian confirmed.

"No, sir."

"And Mr. Hutchinson, in all that video, did you see anything that indicated this murder was related to a gang turf war or a robbery gone bad?"

Again, Hutchinson thought for a moment. Again, he answered, "No, nothing like that."

"Thank you, Mr. Hutchinson," Khachaturian concluded. "No further questions."

Brunelle didn't re-direct. He was done with Hutchinson.

"The State recalls Detective Emory."

CHAPTER 33

Brunelle strode out to the hallway even as Khachaturian, Judge Nguyen, and probably even Carlisle, wondered why he was recalling the lead detective. Hutchinson was the logical end point. But he wouldn't close the deal. The jury needed someone they could trust. Someone they could like. And Emory was pretty damn likeable.

"Thank you for returning, Det. Emory," Brunelle got right to it. "I want to direct your attention to the video footage from the garage that night."

"Okay," Emory replied.

Brunelle turned the projector back on, but this time removed the DMV photo. That left just the still from the surveillance video. The dark, gritty image of the person everyone agreed murdered Gerald Jenkins in cold blood. The only dispute was whether the man in the image was Neil Rappaport.

"Did you personally view the video footage that night?"

"Yes, I did," Emory answered.

Brunelle knew he had to be careful. She couldn't say the magic word. So he told her not to.

"Don't tell me whether you identified the person in the video." He looked up at the screen. "The person in that image right there. But you did watch it, correct?"

"Correct."

"And—this is a yes or no question—did you believe you recognized the person in the video?"

Emory thought for a moment, then nodded slowly, and tentatively answered, "Yes."

Brunelle stole a glance over at Khachaturian. He was tensed, ready to object the moment Emory said the name of the person she 'recognized', as opposed to identified.

So Brunelle didn't ask that question.

"So what did you do next?"

Emory thought for a moment, then smiled slightly. She turned to the jury. "I drove out and arrested the defendant, Neil Rappaport, for the murder of Gerald Jenkins."

Brunelle allowed himself a slight smile too. He really did like Emory. She read him.

"And what did he say when you told him that?"

Emory turned again to the jury and repeated exactly what Brunelle had told them at the beginning of the trial. "He said, 'I don't know who that is.'"

Brunelle had no further questions. Khachaturian couldn't cross on the 'recognition' and resultant actions without giving Emory a chance to expound on how she was able to recognize his client, so there was no cross-examination at all. Emory stepped down and Brunelle stood up.

"The State rests."

CHAPTER 34

"That was pretty slick," Carlisle complimented Brunelle once they were in the hallway, taking the standard recess after the State rested its case-in-chief.

"Do you think the jury got it?" Brunelle asked his partner.

"Oh, they got it," Carlisle confirmed. She turned to Emory, who was standing with them for the debrief. "Good job, Detective."

"Thanks," she replied. Then she shook her head and looked at the ground. "I hope they get it. I hope they hold him responsible for what he did."

"I hope so too," Brunelle answered. "I hope so too."

Emory departed then and Carlisle and Brunelle each went to their respective restrooms. They met back inside Nguyen's courtroom, wondering what might happen next.

"Do you think they'll put him on the stand?" Carlisle asked, referring to Rappaport.

"I don't know," Brunelle replied with a frown. "The jury is going to want to hear him deny the murder, but the judge is going to tell them that his decision not to testify can't be used against him. Khachaturian sure seems to be going for a 'They didn't prove it' defense. If he really thinks that, he doesn't need to put his guy on."

"Especially since he did do it," Carlisle added. "If he admits that, he's convicted, obviously. But if he denies it, the jury might be able to tell he's lying."

Brunelle nodded. "Exactly. Who knows? Maybe they won't put on any case at all and we'll be giving closing arguments first thing tomorrow."

Just then, Khachaturian walked up to them, along with a portly, middle-aged man with thin white hair, thick black-rimmed glasses, and a worn tweed sport coat that had become a size or two too small over the years.

"Mr. Brunelle, Ms. Carlisle," Khachaturian said. "This is our expert, Dr. Peter Grimwald."

"Expert?" Brunelle and Carlisle both replied in unison.

"You didn't endorse any experts," Carlisle complained even as Brunelle asked, "Expert in what?"

"Eyewitness identification," Khachaturian answered Brunelle's question first, before addressing Carlisle's complaint. "We're the defense, Ms. Carlisle. We're not required to disclose witnesses until we decide to call them, and we don't have to make that decision until after the State has put on its case. Mr. Rappaport is presumed innocent. We don't have to prove anything. But we might decide to rebut something you've put on, after you've put it on."

Brunelle didn't necessarily agree with that interpretation of the court rules. But he was guessing that, after expressing some irritation at the late notice, Judge Nguyen was probably going to allow the defense to put on whatever case they wanted to. That was the safest thing to do for the appeal—although there would only be an appeal if there was a conviction. Still, there was a prejudice in favor of allowing defendants facing decades in a cage to put on their case. At most, they'd be given an opportunity to interview Grimwald prior to his testimony.

"Eyewitness identification?" Brunelle repeated. "And what are you going to testify about in this case, Dr. Grimwald?"

Khachaturian answered for him. "He's going to explain how people identify faces and why eyewitness identification of criminal suspects is problematic and unreliable."

"Is that right, Doctor?" Brunelle asked him directly.

"Yes," Grimwald agreed. "That's correct."

"So you don't think Mr. Rappaport could have been identified from the video?"

"I think," Grimwald answered, "that eyewitness identification is not very reliable, and I will explain to the jury why not."

Brunelle nodded and forced a smile. "Great. Awesome. Thanks." He looked to Khachaturian. "You know we're going to object to the late notice, right?"

But Khachaturian just grinned back at him. "You know you're going to lose that objection, right?"

Brunelle did know it. So he just nodded and smiled again. "Nice to meet you. Dr. Grimwald."

Judge Nguyen took the bench shortly thereafter and went on the record with the attorneys before bringing the jury back out.

"Does the defense plan to call any witnesses, Mr. Khachaturian?" she asked. "To include Mr. Rappaport?"

Khachaturian stood up. "The defense plans to call one witness, Your Honor. Dr. Peter Grimwald, who is an expert on eyewitness identification."

"And the State is objecting to this witness, Your Honor," Carlisle jumped up to interject. "We were given no notice. We have received no reports. We—"

"Hold on, Ms. Carlisle," Judge Nguyen interrupted. "You'll get your chance to speak. But I'd like to hear first from Mr. Khachaturian." She turned to the defense attorney. "So, just Dr. Grimwald, then? No other defense witnesses?"

"No other witnesses," Khachaturian confirmed.

"Okay." The judge looked back to Carlisle. "And the State is objecting, Ms. Carlisle?"

"Yes, Your Honor," she answered. "We were given no notice of this witness." She picked up her book of court rules, already opened up to the relevant provision. "Criminal Rule 4.7(b)(1) states clearly, 'the defendant shall disclose to the prosecuting attorney, no later than the omnibus hearing, the names and addresses of persons whom the defendant intends to call as witnesses at the trial.' Further, Rule 4.7(g) states, 'the court may require the defendant to disclose any statements or reports of experts which the defendant intends to use at trial.'"

She set the rulebook down again. "We just learned of this witness during the recess, Your Honor. We had no notice, and we have received no reports from this alleged expert in eyewitness identification. This is a clear violation of the discovery rules, and the court should exclude the witness."

Judge Nguyen acknowledged the argument with a nod. "Any response, Mr. Khachaturian?"

"We have complied with the discovery rules, Your Honor," Khachaturian insisted. "The rule requires us to inform the prosecution as soon as we intend to call the witness. We didn't make the decision to call this particular witness until Mr. Brunelle pulled his little 'recognition but not identification' trick with the final witness. As soon as we made that decision, we informed the prosecution."

Nguyen raised an eyebrow. "You don't expect me to believe

that you found Dr. Grimwald in just the last thirty minutes, do you? You obviously had already retained his services and anticipated at least the possibility of calling him as a witness in this trial."

"Of course, Your Honor," Khachaturian admitted. "But possibility is not actuality. We advised the State of our witness as soon as we made the decision to call him. We can't give any more notice than that."

Nguyen frowned. She looked back at the prosecutors. "Do you want to be heard on this, Mr. Brunelle?"

Brunelle stood up. "No, Your Honor. I believe Ms. Carlisle has expressed our position very well. Thank you."

Nguyen's frown remained as she turned back to Khachaturian. "This sure seems like sandbagging, Mr. Khachaturian. I mean, I assume your witness knew to come to court today because you had already told him you were going to call him as a witness?"

Before Khachaturian could reply, Harold Voegel stood to address the court. Brunelle had almost forgotten he was there. "If I may respond, Your Honor?"

Nguyen appeared equally surprised, but she quickly agreed, "Of course. Go ahead."

"Thank you," Voegel answered. "Miss Carlisle misreads the rule, Your Honor. She is trying to make it say more than it does. We have complied with the letter of the court rule and that is all we have to do. The Court should not expand our obligations and find a violation of some alleged 'spirit' of the rule. There are no spirits to rules. There are only words, and we have complied with those words. We need do nothing more. And might I add," he looked sidelong at the prosecution table, "the prosecutors are two experienced trial attorneys who should be able to deal with unexpected events and adjust accordingly. It's unseemly that they should complain to the Court about how unfair the rules are. They should play by the rules and win or lose by those rules."

Nguyen smiled slightly at the harangue. Brunelle and Carlisle did not. But they didn't have anything to add to their argument.

"I'm going to allow Dr. Grimwald to testify," Judge Nguyen ruled to the surprise of no one, but the visible consternation of Carlisle. "Does the prosecution want time to interview him prior to his testimony?"

That seemed like a good idea to Brunelle, but Carlisle answered for them without even looking at him. "No, Your Honor, that won't be necessary."

Judge Nguyen raised another eyebrow, but like any other judge, she was happy to keep things moving. "Then let's bring in the jury."

As the bailiff set to that task, Brunelle leaned over and whispered to Carlisle. "Are you sure we shouldn't interview him first?"

"Pfft. Why?" Carlisle scoffed. "We know what he's going to say." She pulled out her phone. "I'm not going to interview him. I'm going to Google him. If there's any dirt on him, that's where I'll find it."

Soon the jury was seated and Judge Nguyen formally asked, "Does the defense wish to call any witnesses?"

"Yes, Your Honor," Khachaturian answered. "The defense calls Dr. Peter Grimwald."

Grimwald had taken a seat in the gallery just behind the defense table. He rose and approached the witness stand, where Judge Nguyen swore him in and he sat down to begin his testimony.

"Please state your name, sir," Khachaturian began the direct.

"Peter Grimwald. G-R-I-M-W-A-L-D."

"How are you employed, sir?"

"I am an associate professor of psychology at Washington Technical University."

"Do you hold any degrees relevant to that position?" Khachaturian continued.

"I have a Bachelor of Arts in Philosophy from Washington State University," Grimwald answered, "and a Ph.D. in Applied Psychology from Great Lakes University in Hamilton, Michigan."

"How long have you been teaching at Washington Tech?" Khachaturian asked.

"It will be twenty-two years next fall," Grimwald answered proudly.

"Do you have any particular areas of interest or expertise?" Khachaturian asked, knowing the answer damn well.

"Yes," Grimwald said. "My area of focus is sensory perception and processing, and the ways in which the mind accepts, integrates, modifies, and stores data."

"Now you just said 'modifies,'" Khachaturian pointed out. "Do our minds sometimes modify information before storing it?"

"Oh yes," Grimwald answered. "That's why people often remember events as much better or much worse than they actually were at the time. In fact, the modification can continue as new information is added. For instance, you might have gotten very angry at someone, say in an argument, but if you later become good friends with that person, you may forget how angry you were. In fact, you may forget the argument altogether."

"Interesting, interesting," Khachaturian responded. "Now, are you familiar with any research on how these phenomena might impact criminal investigations?"

"Yes, I am very familiar with such research," Grimwald

replied.

"And specifically," Khachaturian went on, "are you familiar with any research about the reliability of eyewitness identification of criminal suspects?"

"I am familiar with that research," Grimwald confirmed.

"And what does that research show us?"

"That eyewitnesses are usually wrong," Grimwald declared. "At least when it comes to identifying suspects in a crime."

"Really?" Khachaturian mimicked shock. "Now, that seems surprising to me. Should it be?"

"It's not surprising if you understand how the human brain works," Grimwald answered. "And especially how recognition works. Our brains aren't computers and our eyes aren't cameras. We don't record things exactly as they are. Instead, we are social animals, and we process information in the context of what is most advantageous for us socially. I don't need to be able to remember every detail of my wife's face to know it's my wife when I see her. It would be very strange if every time we got together, I examined her face to ensure that it matched the face I saw last time. That's not how recognition works."

He reached into his pocket and pulled out a coin.

"The classic example is a penny. If I asked you to draw a penny from memory, you wouldn't get all the details right. You might have Abe Lincoln facing the wrong way, and you almost certainly wouldn't remember what words went where. But if I show you a penny, you recognize it. And if it was counterfeit and good old Abe was facing the wrong way, you notice that instantly."

"Well, that's all very interesting," Khachaturian said, "but what does that have to do with eyewitness identification of criminal suspects?"

"Well, with eyewitnesses," Grimwald explained, "we're

asking them to recognize someone based on entirely insufficient data. The reason I recognize my wife, or you recognize a real penny, is because we've seen those things so many times over our lives. But your typical eyewitness only catches a glimpse of the perpetrator, usually from a distance, and maybe only the side of the face. And then they're asked whether they recognize a particular suspect. Now, the honest answer should always be no, but again, there are social aspects to all this which impact how our brains work. When an authority figure asks you to do something, your natural inclination is to do it. That's good when it's stopping for children in a crosswalk, but it's bad when it's identifying a suspect that, in reality, you can't possibly identify. You want to please the authority figure, and so your brain modifies that information it has and suddenly you think you do recognize that person you saw for one second, a hundred feet away, as they ran past wearing a hat and sunglasses. You aren't lying, but you aren't correct either."

Khachaturian nodded. "Then why do the police still rely on eyewitness identifications?"

"Well, there are two answers to that," Grimwald replied. "First, what choice do they have? Sometimes the only evidence is the word of an eyewitness, and they have societal pressures to do their job and catch the bad guys. Second, there is actually a growing trend to move away from reliance on eyewitness identification and rely more on physical evidence like DNA. There's a growing recognition that things like cross-racial identification—where the witness and the suspect are different races—is very, very unreliable, so I think you're going to see more and more law enforcement agencies move away from reliance on eyewitness identification."

"Thank you, Doctor," Khachaturian said as he switched gears slightly. "Now I'd like to talk about this case in particular. Have you had a chance to review the video in this case?"

"I have."

Carlisle sneered. "Sure, during that twenty-minute break," she hissed under her breath.

"And do you have an opinion as to whether there is sufficient information in that video for anyone to identify the alleged shooter?"

"Yes," Grimwald answered. "In my opinion, there is not enough information to reliably identify the alleged shooter."

"And why is that?"

"It's a very brief glimpse, it's from a distance, it's from an unusual angle, and the resolution is considerably less than the naked human eye," Grimwald explained. "For a reliable identification, you would want a full and extended view of the person's entire face. You simply don't have that here. It's not enough."

Khachaturian smiled at his witness. "Thank you, Doctor. I don't have any other questions."

"Do you want me--?" Brunelle started to ask Carlisle, but she stuck a hand out at him and sprang to her feet.

"I got this."

"So, Dr. Grimwald," she almost growled as she stalked her way toward the witness stand, "you're saying that the lead detective on this case can't possibly have recognized your client, Mr. Rappaport, because she's Black, is that right?"

"What?" Grimwald replied. "No, I didn't say that."

"You said that Detective Casey Emory, a lead detective in the violent crimes unit of the Bellevue Police Department—a woman who has dedicated her career to protecting our community—is mentally incapable of recognizing a semi-famous tech industry celebrity because she's Black."

"I did not say that," Grimwald defended.

"You said cross-racial identification is unreliable," Carlisle reminded him.

"It is," Grimwald insisted.

"And so the Black detective can't identify the White murderer, is that it?"

"I didn't say that!"

"Have you ever met Det. Emory?" Carlisle asked.

"No," Grimwald replied. "No, I haven't."

"Do you know anything about her?"

"I—No. I don't know anything about her."

"Do you know how long she's been a police officer? Do you know how many hours a week she works? Do you know how many trainings she's attended? Do you know what gets her out of bed every morning to literally risk her life for you, me, and everyone else in our community?"

"No. No, I don't know any of that."

She pointed behind her at Rappaport but kept her gaze locked on Grimwald. "Then how dare you say she can't identify that man right over there as the one who murdered Gerald Jenkins?"

"I—I'm just saying—" he tried.

"How dare you?" Carlisle demanded again.

Khachaturian stood up. "Objection, Your Honor. Counsel is badgering the witness."

"Sustained," Judge Nguyen ruled.

Carlisle didn't apologize. She didn't withdraw the question. She didn't rephrase. She just looked disgustedly at Grimwald, and turned her back on him. "No further questions."

Khachaturian didn't try to rehabilitate. He wasn't going to touch that. He'd made his point. Carlisle had made hers.

"No further questions," he said. "And no further witnesses.

The defense rests."

"All right then," Judge Nguyen told the jurors. "That concludes the evidence in the case. We will adjourn for the day and reconvene in the morning for closing arguments."

The jury filed out of the courtroom and Judge Nguyen retired to chambers.

Once they were gone, Brunelle looked at Carlisle. "Uh, wow. That was pretty aggressive."

Carlisle smiled. "Yeah, I know. And it was fun." She looked over at Grimwald who was whispering with Khachaturian and Rappaport, with Voegel and Walker listening in. "You know what the best part is?"

"What?" Brunelle asked.

She held up her phone. "Grimwald was right. There's all kinds of research that our brains prioritize what to remember. And you know what we remember most? Conflict. And danger. The only thing any of those jurors are going to remember about Grimwald's testimony is that crazy bitch prosecutor calling him a racist."

She put her phone back in her pocket and picked up her briefcase. "Now, come on. Let's go get drunk."

CHAPTER 35

Brunelle didn't actually want to get drunk. But they did need to debrief, and it had been a long day, a long trial. He was willing to share a drink with a colleague as they discussed her closing argument. And there was a restaurant a few blocks from the courthouse that had good food and a decent bartender. Within an hour, they were parked at a corner table, drinks in hand and burgers on their way.

"I have to hand it to Khachaturian," Brunelle said. "He really put the knife in us about there being no motive. And he kept twisting. Not only did he point out that Rappaport had no motive, he elicited what the most common motives were so the jury would see none of those applied to him either."

"Yeah, that didn't help us," Carlisle agreed. "But we're handling it as best we can. If there's no motive, then maybe that's the motive. Just random violence for violence's sake."

Brunelle frowned. "That almost never happens though. I've been doing this for over twenty years, and I've never seen someone kill someone else for no reason."

"What did Kaladi say?" Carlisle recalled. "Love or money,

right?"

But Brunelle shook his head. "No, it's usually drugs or alcohol. I think ninety percent of the cases I've ever done have been drug-related. Using drugs, buying drugs, stealing to pay for the drugs, and of course, getting into fights because you're on drugs."

"Well," Carlisle raised her glass, "don't people maybe use drugs and alcohol to approximate the feeling you get from love?"

"Or from money," Brunelle joked. "That's got to be a nice feeling."

"Or both," Carlisle suggested.

Brunelle nodded. "Yeah." He ran a finger over the last of the cuts on his face. "That's what happened to me, actually. I got on the wrong side of a guy who was looking for both and thought I was in the way."

"Oh, yeah?" Carlisle said. "I've been dying to ask, but you really didn't want to talk about it."

"I didn't," Brunelle laughed. "But I guess maybe it's proof that people will commit violence for love and/or money."

"So, what was the story?" Carlisle asked over another sip of her drink. "How did beating your ass get this guy love or money?"

"First of all," Brunelle answered after his own sip, "it was three guys. But the main guy thought he was gonna get rich if he got with Vickie. So he wanted me out of the picture."

"You already were out of the picture," Carlisle said.

"Yeah, I pointed that out. He didn't believe me. It wasn't until I explained that he wasn't going to get rich with Vickie that he decided maybe I wasn't worth assaulting any more."

"Wait," Carlisle responded. "I thought Vickie was loaded. Didn't she get a huge divorce settlement or something?"

Brunelle shook his head. "No. It's really complicated. Partnership agreements, lawsuits, alimony. Just a big mess."

"What? Not love, money, and drugs?"

Brunelle was about to say 'No,' but he stopped. He thought for a moment. And he finally understood.

Carlisle saw the expression on his face. "What?"

"I get it," he said. "I know why he did it."

"The guy who kicked your ass?"

"No," Brunelle answered. "Rappaport. I know why he did it."

CHAPTER 36

The next morning, everyone was ready for closing arguments. But Brunelle and Carlisle had other plans.

It had taken three tries before Paul answered Brunelle's call. It took another twenty minutes and intervention from Carlisle to convince him to show up at the courtroom the next morning. And a combination of begging, promises, and a veiled threat of subpoenas and arrest to get him to agree to bring Vickie with him.

And that was nothing compared to what it was going to take to convince Judge Nguyen to let them put on two more witnesses. Including the one witness Brunelle had agreed not to call.

"Ready for closing arguments, Mr. Brunelle and Ms. Carlisle?" Khachaturian asked as he arrived, in a rare show of collegiality. "I certainly am." Or not.

"Yeah," Brunelle responded, "about that…"

But before he could explain more, Judge Nguyen took the bench. She echoed Khachaturian's question/taunt. "Are the parties ready for closing arguments this morning?"

The prosecutor always went first. Brunelle looked up at the judge. "Actually, Your Honor, the State would like to put on a rebuttal case."

Nguyen gave a thoughtful expression. Rebuttal cases were allowed. Not common, but permitted. "Okay. Do you have an expert to respond to Dr. Grimwald?"

Brunelle shrugged his shoulders noncommittally. "Not exactly, Your Honor. We have two civilians we'd like to call."

The judge's eyes narrowed. Brunelle didn't even want to see Khachaturian's expression. Well, actually, he kind of did. But he was focused on Judge Nguyen.

"And who might that be?" Judge Nguyen asked. Her expression suggested she suspected something was up.

Brunelle smiled weakly. "Paul Cross and Victoria Cross."

"What?" Khachaturian slammed the table as he jumped to his feet. "Objection, Your Honor. We object. Mr. Brunelle specifically agreed not to call Victoria Cross as a witness. We relied on that promise. We withdrew our motion based on that promise. We built our case based on that promise."

"You called one witness," Brunelle pointed out.

"All comments addressed to me," Judge Nguyen put in, lest she lose control of the argument. "And Mr. Brunelle, don't interrupt."

She motioned for Khachaturian to continue.

"We relied on that agreement, Your Honor," Khachaturian repeated. "You should hold them to it."

Carlisle stood up to respond. She had made Brunelle promise she could respond.

"Well, Your Honor," she said when the judge asked for a response. "The agreement was actually that we wouldn't call Ms. Cross in our case-in-chief. But this is rebuttal. We rested our case-in-chief without calling her. We honored the letter of our agreement. And the Court should not seek out some 'spirit' of that agreement.

There is no spirit to the agreement, only the words. And we honored those words."

Khachaturian looked down at Voegel. Voegel scowled but didn't say anything.

"And if I might say so," Carlisle added, "the defense team are experienced lawyers. They should be able to deal with unexpected events and adjust accordingly."

Judge Nguyen nodded. "I remember the stipulation. And I remember that it only included the State's case-in-chief. I noted it at the time, but didn't comment. It's not my role to influence agreements between the parties. Ms. Carlisle is correct, the agreement doesn't preclude calling these witnesses. But," she raised a cautious finger, "this is rebuttal, not an extension of your case-in-chief. Do these witnesses rebut Dr. Grimwald somehow?" she asked.

"Oh, yes, Your Honor," Carlisle assured.

"Do they also have Ph.D.s in applied psychology?" the judge asked dubiously.

"Well, no," Carlisle admitted. "But they will be able to rebut Dr. Grimwald's assertion that Mr. Rappaport could not have been identified from the video."

Judge Nguyen sighed. She thought for a few moments. Then she looked over at Khachaturian and his co-counsel. "Anything further from the defense?"

But Khachaturian just repeated, "We object, Your Honor, for the reasons we already stated."

So, no, Brunelle thought. *Nothing further from the defense.*

Judge Nguyen chewed on her cheek for several seconds. Then she nodded. "I'm going to allow the State to call the witnesses. I gave the defense some slack when they sprang Dr. Grimwald on the prosecution with essentially no notice. I will extend the same courtesy to the State. Mr. Voegel, and Ms. Carlisle, are right. Unexpected things happen in trial. That's part of why we have them."

She turned to her bailiff. "Bring in the jury."

Then to Brunelle and Carlisle. "And bring in your first witness."

Vickie was first. And Carlisle did the examination. Obviously.

"Could you please state your name for the record?"

Vickie had come to court, she was clearly not happy about it. But she'd dressed to the nines—not at Brunelle, surely—and commanded the room from the witness stand. Even more so when she told the jury her name.

"Victoria Cross. Formerly Victoria Rappaport."

"So, you know the defendant?" Carlisle asked.

"Yes," Vickie confirmed. "He's my ex-husband."

"When did you get divorced?"

Vickie thought for a moment. "It's been several months now."

"In relation to the murder at issue in this case," Carlisle clarified her inquiry, "when did the divorce become final?"

"It became final the Friday before the murder."

"Less than a week?"

"Less than a week," Vickie confirmed.

She was answering the questions, but she refused to look at Brunelle. Somehow, Brunelle was okay with that. Carlisle continued.

"What were the terms of your divorce settlement? Did you receive any equity in RapTech?"

"No," Vickie answered. "I agreed to a monthly alimony amount instead."

Carlisle cocked her head. "Why would you agree to that?"

"Because he threatened to fight for fifty percent custody of the kids if I didn't take it," Vickie explained, "but offered he would only see them two weekends a month if I accepted his terms and let the divorce go through as soon as the ninety-day waiting period ended."

"And did it go through then?"

"Yes," Vickie confirmed. "The divorce became final exactly ninety days after he served me with the divorce papers."

"And less than a week later, Gerald Jenkins was murdered?"

Vicki shrugged. "I guess so. Yes."

Carlisle nodded to her. "Thank you, Ms. Cross. No further questions.

All eyes turned to Khachaturian. He stood up slowly, almost tentatively.

"Good morning, Ms. Cross," he began. "I only have a few questions."

Vickie gave a curt nod. "Good."

"You were not in the parking garage on the night of the murder, correct?"

"Correct," Vickie answered.

"You did not see the murder, correct?"

Again, "Correct."

"So you don't know who murdered Gerald Jenkins?"

She shook her head. "No, I don't."

"Do you even know who Gerald Jenkins is?"

Another shake of the head. "No, I'm afraid I don't."

Khachaturian nodded. "Thank you, Ms. Cross. I don't have any further questions."

Carlisle didn't either, and Victoria Cross stalked out of the courtroom, still never looking Brunelle's way. That was just as well;

he was preparing for the next witness. The final witness.

"The State calls Paul Cross," he announced.

Paul seemed less hostile than Vickie, but he still exuded discomfort as he was sworn in and took the stand. Brunelle had him start with his name, and then got right to it.

"Do you know the defendant, Neil Rappaport?"

"Yes," Paul answered.

"How do you know him?"

"He's my business partner," Paul explained. "We founded RapTech together."

"Not CrossTech?" Brunelle asked.

Paul smiled weakly. "Afraid not."

"Is RapTech publicly traded? Or do you and Mr. Rappaport still own the company yourselves?"

"It's privately held," Paul confirmed. "We set it up fifty-fifty when we drafted the partnership agreement, and we still each own a fifty percent share." Then he added, "For now."

So Brunelle followed up. He was going to ask about it anyway. "What does that mean?"

"It means there's a provision in the agreement that if either of us dies or becomes incapacitated, that partner's fifty percent transfers directly to the other partner. It was for tax purposes originally, but it's become an issue recently."

"Oh?" Brunelle asked as if he didn't already know the answer. "How is that?"

Paul sighed and frowned. "About six months ago, Neil started trying to force me out of the company. First, he asked me to sell. Then he filed a lawsuit, but it was thrown out. Then..." but he trailed off.

"Then what?" Brunelle prompted.

"Then he filed for divorce from Vickie," Paul answered.

"Vickie is my sister. He told me he'd call off the divorce if I agreed to sell to him."

"And did you agree?"

Paul's frown deepened. "You know, I might have. Vickie was devastated. But I never got the chance. She was also hurt and angry. She didn't want to be married to someone who didn't want to be with her. So it became moot."

Ok, Brunelle thought to himself, *that's the setup.* He took a deep breath. This wasn't going to be pleasant.

"You're a drug addict, right, Paul?" he suddenly asked.

Paul's jaw dropped. "What?"

"You're a drug addict, right?" Brunelle repeated. "Pills, right?"

"I—I'm not—" Paul looked around the courtroom. It wasn't the best place for an intervention. "I'm not a drug addict."

"I was at the party, Paul," Brunelle reminded him. He didn't reply.

"You had to buy your drugs from somewhere," Brunelle went on. "Jerry Jenkins was your supplier, wasn't he?"

"No," Paul said in a way that didn't convince anyone.

"You can't really hide that kind of thing from everyone, though, can you? Especially not from a business partner you've known for over two decades. That's why he wanted you out, isn't it?"

"He wanted me out," Paul shot back, "because he's a greedy S.O.B. who took all the credit for everyone else's hard work."

"He knew you were buying drugs," Brunelle repeated, "didn't he?"

Paul just stared at Brunelle for several seconds, then he turned away. "Yes."

"And you usually bought them from Gerald Jenkins at that

parking garage, didn't you?"

Paul kept his eyes down. "I only knew him as Jerry. And we would meet different places. But yeah, that was our main place."

Almost there. Time to bring it home.

"You own a black Audi sedan, don't you?"

Paul finally looked back up at Brunelle. "Yeah, I do."

"And if that had been *you*," Brunelle pulled it together, "sitting in *your* identical black Audi, waiting for Jerry, when Neil Rappaport snuck up behind *you* and shot *you* twice in the head, he would have taken one-hundred percent control of RapTech and his newly ex-wife wouldn't be entitled to any of it. Isn't that right?"

Paul's eyes widened. He looked past Brunelle at his business partner and former brother-in-law. "Oh my God. Yes. That's exactly what would have happened."

"Love and money," Brunelle said. "And drugs."

He looked up to Judge Nguyen. "No further questions."

Khachaturian looked like he'd seen a ghost. Or, worse, a conviction. "Uh, could we, Your Honor, could we have a brief recess?"

Judge Nguyen shook her head. "No. Cross-examination. Do you have any questions for Mr. Cross?"

Khachaturian hesitated. He consulted with Voegel and Walker. He tried to consult with Rappaport, but he had dropped his head and wouldn't respond to his attorneys' prodding. Finally, Khachaturian looked up again at Judge Nguyen. "No questions, Your Honor. We have no questions."

And neither did anyone else in the courtroom.

EPILOGUE

Khachaturian got that recess after all, once Paul Cross left the courtroom. He used it to ask Brunelle and Carlisle to recommend the low end of the sentencing range if Rappaport agreed to plead guilty. Actually, he started by asking if they'd amend down to Murder Two. The low end sentencing offer came after Brunelle said no. Actually, it was Carlisle who said it first, and it was preceded by a 'fuck.'

As the jury waited in the jury room, Judge Nguyen went through the guilty plea form with Rappaport, Khachaturian at his side, and Brunelle and Carlisle on the opposite end of the bar. She accepted his plea and followed the sentencing recommendation. Twenty-five years in prison. Not enough, as Beverly Jenkins told the judge before the sentence was imposed.

When the jury was brought back out, Rappaport was gone, already taken away to begin his sentence. The judge explained what had happened. They weren't surprised—they'd heard Paul Cross's testimony too—although several seemed disappointed. They'd sat through an entire trial for nothing. Or almost nothing. Unexpected events happened during the trial, and the lawyers had adjusted accordingly.

As Brunelle and Carlisle departed the courtroom, Khachaturian congratulated them, the Jenkinses thanked them, and Paul Cross avoided them. But Vickie Cross was waiting in the hallway. Waiting for Brunelle.

"Dave," she said. "Can we talk?"

Carlisle stepped to the side. "I'm gonna head upstairs and take all the credit for our victory," she said. "Take your time."

She slipped away and in a moment, Brunelle and Vickie were alone in the hallway.

Vickie spoke first. "Thank you. You held him responsible. I know I should be sad, he's the father of my kids, but what he did... To me. To that man. What he wanted to do to Paul." She shook her head. "So, yeah, just... thank you."

Brunelle demurred. "I was just doing my job."

"Well, you do it very well. I'm sorry I called you a coward. You're not a coward. You didn't give up. You fought to the end and you figured it out and you won. Cowards don't do that."

Brunelle shrugged. "You helped. You and Paul. I couldn't have done it without you."

"Well, don't worry about Paul," Vickie said. "We'll get him into treatment, the best money can buy. Especially after he gets full control of the company."

"What are you going to do now?" Brunelle asked.

Vickie sighed. "I don't know. Go back to work, I guess. Figure out what I want to do. Figure out who I am."

"Once you figure out who you are," Brunelle said, "can I be that person's friend?"

Vickie smiled. Then she grabbed and hugged him. "You already are."

END

THE DAVID BRUNELLE LEGAL THRILLERS
Presumption of Innocence
Tribal Court
By Reason of Insanity
A Prosecutor for the Defense
Substantial Risk
Corpus Delicti
Accomplice Liability
A Lack of Motive
Missing Witness
Diminished Capacity
Devil's Plea Bargain
Homicide in Berlin
Premeditated Intent
Alibi Defense

THE TALON WINTER LEGAL THRILLERS
Winter's Law
Winter's Chance
Winter's Reason
Winter's Justice
Winter's Duty
Winter's Passion

ALSO BY STEPHEN PENNER
Scottish Rite
Blood Rite
Last Rite
Mars Station Alpha
The Godling Club

ABOUT THE AUTHOR

Stephen Penner is an attorney, author, and artist from Seattle.

In addition to writing the *David Brunelle Legal Thriller Series*, he is also the author of the *Talon Winter Legal Thrillers*, starring Tacoma criminal defense attorney Talon Winter; the *Maggie Devereaux Paranormal Mysteries*, recounting the exploits of an American graduate student in the magical Highlands of Scotland; and several stand-alone works.

For more information, please visit *www.stephenpenner.com*.

Made in the USA
Las Vegas, NV
26 September 2022

55966626R00127